Alongside Lucy

Maria Secoy

All Write Well LLC

Romantic Suspense Fiction

Taylor Industries:

Rural romantic suspense with international intrigue
Linked Hearts
Encrypted Hearts
Tracking Hearts
Guarded Hearts
Auditing Hearts
Hacking Hearts

Twisted Willow:

Small town romantic suspense full of action & adventure
Gloria's Gumption
According to Cora
Beth's Absolution
Letting in Liz

On-Trail Love Adventure:

Romantic suspense on the Appalachian Trail
Alongside Lucy
Standing by Stephanie
Crossing with Kiara

Contents

Dedicated

Dedicated to my husband, who cooked dinner all the nights I hid away to write this story. He understands that dog floor on the carpet means, 'It's time to vacuum,' and does just that without hesitation. When he sees the trash is full, he takes it out, because he gets that we're equal partners. I can't imagine doing life with anyone else.

Chapter 1

LUCY

Pain shot up Lucy's right shin with every step as she climbed away from Vermont Route Nine. Six hundred miles from Harper's Ferry, and her body was starting to rebel.

"Stupid question," she muttered, still annoyed by the shuttle driver's parting words. *Are you sure you're going to be okay out there by yourself?* It was like she hadn't already proven herself by covering more than six-hundred miles of the Appalachian Trail.

The July heat pressed down through the canopy, but at least the shade felt better than the blazing asphalt she'd left behind. A bright orange salamander darted across the path. Red efts, though why they called the orange ones "red" was beyond her. She stepped carefully around it and kept climbing.

By the time she'd cleared the steep ascent out of Bennington, her shin felt like someone was driving hot nails through the bone. Just when she was seriously contemplating the benefits of a prosthetic leg, she spotted the blue blazes leading to the shelter.

She could have cried with relief.

Lucy followed the side trail, already planning her routine. She liked to get her water first before her legs stiffened up. Then she'd sit, cook, eat, and relax. Maybe she'd actually get to eat lunch without her leg screaming at her.

But as she approached the three-sided structure, she noticed another pack and trekking poles leaning against the platform. The sight deflated her hopes. She'd hoped for solitude to nurse her injury and figure out whether she could keep going or needed to bail.

Lucy dropped her pack onto the picnic table bench and dug out her bear canister. The solid black Garcia had saved her from learning the hard way about proper food storage. She was just setting up her stove when footsteps approached from behind the shelter.

"Hey, I thought I heard somebody else pulling in."

Lucy looked up to see a clean-shaven hiker emerging with a freshly filled water bottle. No scraggly trail beard, no funky hiker stench. This was unusual for someone this deep in the wilderness. He had a sharp jawline and shaggy hair, and he actually looked like he might have showered sometime in the past week.

"Yeah, this is my lunch stop." She tried not to stare while wondering if he planned to take his shirt off in the heat.

Lightning shot up her shin again as she stepped around the table to find level ground for her fuel canister. It was time for more ibuprofen. "You okay?" the guy was frowning at her and had brushed his sun-bleached locks away from his face revealing his bright, emerald eyes. "I'm Jacks by the way."

"Oh, yeah, I'm Loner. I'll be fine. I'm just fighting through shin splints right now." Like other hikers, Lucy always used her trail name instead of her real name when meeting random people out in the woods. She wondered if Jacks was his real name or the moniker he went by on the trail and decided to ask him about it as she popped two painkillers into her mouth.

His smile made her flutter inside in a way that she hadn't since early on in her marriage. Her late husband had been gone for almost two years now, and while she had no interest in trying to replace him, Jacks was a pleasure to look at.

"I'm a sports therapist back in civilization if you'd like me to look at it. A bit of massage can really help a lot. We can swap trail name stories while I check it out."

He didn't step any closer to her. Lucy's insides battled. She hadn't felt the contact of another human's skin on hers in a long time. Of course, she got lots of hugs and an occasional pat on the back, but having someone rub, touch, and feel her skin... that wasn't something she had experienced since her husband's car accident. She hadn't really missed it until right then, either.

Of course, now that she was thinking about it, it sounded like the best thing on earth. Except, she hadn't shaved her legs for more than a month, and she wasn't entirely sure she wouldn't freak out the second he touched her.

Jacks could see her debate. "If it helps any, the massage will likely hurt at first, but your leg will feel better later, and of course, all you have to do is say the word and I'll stop."

He still hadn't taken a single step toward her, and for some reason, that reassured her. "Ok," she said unsure where to go from there.

He smiled at her again. Not a big grin or a condescending, pity grin, but a friendly smile. "Why don't you sit backwards on the bench, and then you can prop your foot up here on my lap while you lean back against the table."

Suddenly, Lucy remembered her unshaven legs. "Oh, um, I'm thru-hiking and don't bother carrying a razor." Crap, this was embarrassing. She closed her eyes, felt completely stupid and wanted to just disappear under the table where she could hide from her awkwardness until the hot man left.

And then he laughed!

"I kind of figured. I'd have been much more surprised to discover your legs were smooth. I might only be a section hiker, but I've done enough LASHes to be familiar with how this works."

Lucy breathed out, opened her eyes, found his green ones full of kindness, and decided to leap. She pulled off her shoes, peeled off her right sock, rolled up her pantleg, and placed her foot on the platform beside him.

Jacks immediately cupped her heel and shifted her foot between his knees so that both of his hands could reach her calf.

"So, you're a section hiker?" Lucy asked to distract herself from the feel of his hands on her skin.

"Yeah, I can sometimes manage a full month on the trail, but mostly it's a few days here and there. I have completed from Georgia to here, though." He pressed on a knot in her calf, and she had to a stifle a yelp. "Sorry, I wasn't kidding when I said it will hurt along the way but feel much better afterward. Have you been taking painkillers?"

"Oh yeah, Ibuprofen is my friend," Lucy assured him.

And there was that smile again.

"Good. So, trail names." Jacks sighed before starting his story. "I actually started hiking the trail almost ten years ago. I had just graduated college and was planning to thru-hike. I didn't really know the first thing about the trail or backpacking, but... anyway, I found I would get really bored in camp sometimes, so I started carrying a game of jacks with me. I'd sit around camp, bounce the ball, and scoop up jacks most evenings. Soon, everyone started calling me Jacks."

Lucy chuckled. She loved hearing about how people had gotten their names. "So did you finish your thru-hike that year?" she asked him.

Jacks continued to massage the knots in Lucy's calf as he got a wistful look in his eyes, "Nah, my grandmother passed away just before I hit the Smokies. When I was growing up, it was just her and I, though she had tons of friends. Her memorial service was packed." He looked a bit proud of that.

Lucy returned his smile. "I wish loss was easier to deal with, and I'm sorry to hear you lost your person."

"You say that like you know the feeling," Jacks commented.

"Yeah, my husband was hit by a semi sliding across ice. It will have been two years ago this coming November."

Jacks inhaled deeply. "That's awful. Do you have any kids?"

"No, we'd only been married for three years. We weren't even sure we wanted kids." Lucy shrugged. Sometimes the pain of her missing husband hit her with a sharp stab, but now, it was usually a dull ache or the comfort of a fond memory.

"Ok, so how did you end up as 'Loner'?" Jacks asked in an obvious attempt to lighten the mood and return them to friendly conversation.

"It's not obvious?" Lucy asked. "I prefer to hike my own hike and don't really have any interest in finding a tramily."

Sometimes it felt like the Appalachian Trail came with its own language. Hikers were grouped into three categories: Thru-hikers for those covering the entire trail in one season or year; Section hikers were those out for just a few days or a week; and LASHers, or Long Ass Section Hikers, were those who were hiking for several weeks, but not planning to cover the entire trail at once. Thru-hikers and LASHers often ended up seeing the same people day after day. Sometimes they'd split the cost of shuttles into town and plan their days to intentionally make camp together. When a group traveled together for a while, they formed a "tramily," or trail family, that shared deep bonds.

When Jacks hmmed and continued to massage her leg, she added more detail to her story, "When I left Harper's Ferry, I ended up hiking with a few other people. They were nice and friendly and wanted to align our schedules. I just didn't. I like being able to do my own thing. It's a bit selfish, but I don't want to worry about anyone else or their feelings or... anything." Lucy shrugged and winced as Jacks dug into another knot.

"I can see that." He continued to work silently as the birds chirped around them. Lucy could hear a squirrel rustling through the brush somewhere off to her left as she closed her eyes, soaked in the rays of sun hitting her face, and focused on breathing through the bruising pain of Jacks' massage.

After a bit, he shifted to gently rubbing her skin before extending her leg and flexing her toes back toward her knee. "How's that feel?" he asked her.

"Hmm," Lucy took a deep breath in and shook herself from the relaxed, trance-like state she'd found, "Actually, much better. I mean it kinda feels a bit bruised, but it doesn't have that sharp, stabby feeling it did before."

"Good. You might see some bruising appear over the next day or two, but it shouldn't be bad. Be sure to stretch well and often. This isn't a cure or really even a temporary fix, it just helps ease the stress that causes the shin splints. Continue to massage it to try and keep those tight knots from reforming; they add to the stress in your lower legs. I hate to say this, but you should really keep your daily mileage low. How many miles per day are you doing?"

"Ha! Yeah, attempting eighteen to twenty mile days is how I ended up like this. I've already made the adjustment to limit myself to ten to fifteen miles per day," she assured him.

"Good." He openly grinned at her now and her fluttery feeling returned. "How far are you going today?"

"I just got dropped off at VT Nine and am planning to spend the night at Goddard Shelter, so about ten miles total. I've got this stop for lunch and another for dinner before I make camp." With most hikers, Lucy refused to share her planned itinerary.

She'd respond with the vaguest answer she could get away with while still appearing polite and friendly. Something about Jacks struck her differently, though. She didn't even hesitate before telling him her plans.

"Ah, that's where I was last night. It's a nice shelter, though there's not many tent spots. If you get a chance and feel up to it, you should walk down and checkout the old shelter remains. It's still standing and pretty cool to see." Lucy noticed Jacks' cheeks turn red as he hurried to add, "At least, it's cool if you're a bit of dorky nerd like me."

Lucy grinned back at him, "Oh yeah, I love checking out old stuff like that! Did you stop at Mosby Camp in Virginia where that old shelter got stolen?" Lucy stuffed down her disappointment at the realization that he was headed south, reminded herself that she was "Loner" for a reason, and refocused on enjoying their conversation.

Jacks gently lowered her foot to the ground and began unpacking food and setting up his own stove as he replied, "Yes! I was so excited to see it. I mean, how can anyone steal an entire 3-sided building? I was disappointed when I got there, though. Apparently, it's become a local party spot. The whole area was littered with trash. Someone had dumped leftover food right beside the campsite, and there was human poop just beside the best tent spot. It was a few years ago, now, so maybe it's been cleaned up a bit, but I ended up moving on and staying elsewhere that night."

As Lucy stepped around the corner of the table to get her food out of her bear canister, she realized just how much better her leg felt. She closed her eyes, listened to the hiss of her stove, and was grateful for the relief. "Thank you," she told Jacks earnestly.

He gave her a soft look, "I'm glad I could help. My real name's Logan." He turned back to his own food bag and continued rummaging.

"I'm Lucy," she told him.

They continued to talk about nothing while they finished cooking. They swapped trail stories, and Jacks told her about his top-secret tricks to succeed at a game of jacks. She shared her frustration with people always asking if she was okay out here by herself just because she's female. He thought for several moments before verifying that he had never once been asked that question.

As they ate, Lucy couldn't resist asking him about his itinerary.

"Actually," he grinned at her and raised his eyebrows in a teasing way, "I'm only going down to VT Nine and turning around to head back north. This hike's an out-and-back for me. I'm planning to stay at this shelter tonight. How far are you going tomorrow?"

Jacks' hopeful look gave Lucy confidence. "Depending on how my shin feels, I'm thinking I'll end up at either Story Spring Shelter or the campsite near the Daniel Webster Monument."

Jacks smirked at her as he challenged playfully, "I bet I catch up to you tomorrow night."

Lucy laughed, but didn't take the bait, "I bet you do! I'm moving slow, remember?"

Jacks' face fell into a serious expression as he cleaned up his area. "I am glad to hear that you're serious about taking it easy.

I'll keep an eye out for you tomorrow. I can massage the knots out again if you want." He didn't make eye contact as he spoke but nodded at her leg while collecting his things.

Something in his careful attention to her needs, his respectful distance, and the gentle way he spoke about loss made Lucy realize this wasn't just another trail encounter. Here was someone who understood that healing happened slowly, that trust was earned, not demanded. The way he'd shared his own grief without trying to fix hers told her he knew the difference between being alone and being lonely.

Lucy became equally serious as she replied, "Yeah, that would be really nice." She didn't want to hike alone anymore. She could picture the two of them at camp playing jacks together and swapping stories. For the first time since Ben passed, she could see herself spending time with someone else and enjoying it.

Lucy had her things repacked quickly and was physically ready to go before she felt prepared to say farewell to Jacks. She looked around but couldn't find any reason to linger. She still had eight and a half miles to cover and only about six more hours of daylight. It was time to get moving.

"Maybe I'll see you tomorrow," she said to Jacks as she gripped her trekking poles.

"My magic eight ball says that outcome is likely," he joked back before chuckling to himself and adding, "Never mind, I might be more of a nerd than I like to admit. That was super dorky."

Lucy laughed, "It was, but that's okay. Happy Hiking, Logan." She used his real name to try and express her feeling that this meeting was special.

"Same to you Lucy." Apparently, he thought it was special too.

She hiked back up past the blue blazes with a smile on her face.

Chapter 2

LUCY

Lucy checked her bearings to ensure she turned north when she got to the intersection with the Appalachian trail. While no part of the trail was flat, the rest of the day's hike didn't include any climbs as steep as that first mile of her day.

She was able to keep a decent pace as she hiked under a powerline, past a spring that was clearly home to a whole family of frogs, and down a bit of descent to Hell Hollow Brook. It was a nice place to stop, stretch, and refill her water. The footbridge made a pleasant sit-spot, and Lucy leaned back against her pack to relax.

She tilted her head back and listened for the sounds of the forest but realized that she didn't hear them. In fact, she didn't hear anything but the gentle burbling of the creek. She listened harder. The forest was never silent. An eerie feeling crawled up the back of her neck, and she heaved herself up off the ground. She continued to listen as she grabbed her trekking poles from where she had leaned them against a nearby tree.

The intense quiet was creepy.

When Lucy had first started her hike, she'd gotten jumpy easily. She felt like every rustle was a bear and each snapping twig was a crazy psycho out to get her. Over those first few days, she'd learned that loud rustling was always a squirrel and there were fewer crazy psychos to be found in the woods than on a normal trip through Walmart.

This gut feeling of something being wrong was new to her. She reminded herself of all that she had learned along the way, told herself to chill, and started putting one foot in front of the other. She sang to herself to distract her mind and keep it off the crazy train, and soon enough, she realized the normal forest noises had returned. She shook her head and laughed at herself for being so silly.

She was climbing again, but the incline was gentle, and she wasn't in a hurry. She stopped often to stretch her calf.

Normally, she felt the urge to do her business in the morning while she was at camp and near a privy. With today's late start, her digestive system had apparently decided to change up the schedule. Each time she stopped to stretch her calf, she peered around to see if there was a reasonable place for her to venture off the trail to dig a cat hole. She tried to avoid leaving her waste in a six-inch hole in the woods whenever possible, but after spending this much time out here she'd become adept at it even though she didn't like it.

At one point, she looked off to her right and noticed some beautiful purple blossoms peeking out from between some ferns off in the distance. The ground had a gentle slope, and there were many large trees growing in the area. It was the perfect place to count off eighty paces or so and find some privacy behind one of the largest trunks. She'd also have an excuse to get a closer look at the flowers.

Lucy left her pack along the side of the trail with her trekking pole poked in the dirt and her orange bandana tied around the top like a flag waving her back to the path. She grabbed her potty kit and headed off through the brush toward a particularly large tree. When she got to it, she was excited to find a lovely nook tucked into the roots behind the trunk. It was well covered with leaves, but those were easily brushed aside. This kind of space was her ideal natural restroom.

She set her kit down on the ground beside the tree and started to brush the leaves to the side. As she did so, hard, black plastic or metal was revealed. Then some smooth brown parts appeared. These things were clearly man-made and not natural debris, but many people seemed to think that nature was their personal landfill. It wasn't until the trigger guard was exposed that Lucy realized what she was unearthing.

Lucy's late husband had served in the military, and she'd grown up in a family full of hunters, so she was no stranger to guns. That's how she knew that these were not the kinds of rifles used for hunting turkey, raccoon, deer, or even bear. When she finished clearing away the leaves, she counted eight barrels that were clearly attached to the kinds of automatic weapons used by soldiers to hunt humans.

She started to feel a bit dizzy, and her eyes began to water before she realized that she'd stopped blinking or breathing. No normal person had a reason to own these kinds of guns, let alone hide them under a tree out in the woods. Lucy didn't know what they were for, who they belonged to, or why they were here. She did know that they were bad news, and she needed to give them some space.

Lucy brushed the leaves back over the weapons, picked up her bag of supplies and hurriedly moved several yards away. Not wanting to return to the trail and start her search for a suitable spot all over again, she quickly dug a hole, deposited her business, and headed back toward her pack. When she spotted it, she was grateful for the bright orange bandana. In her haste to get away from the guns, she'd covered some distance. She wasn't sure exactly where the guns were, but she didn't want to risk encountering them again, so she made a beeline straight for the trail before hiking along it back to her backpack where she could clean her hands.

After the unexpected discovery, Lucy hadn't taken the time to inspect the pretty purple flowers. Hopefully, there would be more along the trail. She could still see them growing off in the distance, spread out among the trees and ferns. Many of them were almost two feet tall, and she wondered if they were some kind of odd spiderwort and sunflower hybrid. She'd never seen anything like them.

The trail itself had a slight incline at this point, but the further she hiked, the steeper the sides of the trail dropped off. Soon, Lucy crested the ridge. She was still surrounded by trees and still ascending, but she was traveling along the ridgeline now. Just then, she saw a shadow flash through the trees off to her right. She turned, thinking it was a bear, but saw two arms and a head instead. It was gone before she could notice anything more than that. She heard the snap of a branch and the rustle of some leaves but couldn't spot any movement.

Lucy kept walking while she thought about what she'd seen. Why would someone be on the steep hillside and not the trail? Why were they so quick to disappear? Did she even really see anything? Maybe it was a deer or a bear after all. She couldn't dismiss the sounds she heard. They had been fully formed noises that told her it was something big. She was less certain about the glimpse her eyes had captured. Out here, she knew how easy it was for her brain to turn a stick into snake or a stump into a bear.

The more Lucy thought about it, the more she was convinced that it hadn't been anything unusual. By the time she'd reached the top of Little Pond Mountain, she had gone back to enjoying the forest and the beautiful day. The heat of the afternoon was passing, and she was ready for a bite to eat. It hadn't been that long since lunch, but Lucy found that her stomach preferred more small meals while hiking all day.

She found a small clearing where she could lean against the trunk of a tree. She pulled out her sit pad to keep her rear off the dirt and away from bugs. It always amazed her how dry the ground could look while still leaving her with damp britches. She had less than four miles to go, but it was already almost five pm.

With no shelter or picnic table, she chose to enjoy a cold meal that didn't require any preparation. She left her bear canister in her pack but opened the top of it to pull out a squeeze pouch of Justin's almond butter along with a piece of naan. While it was much more common to see hikers pull out tortillas from their pack, Lucy loved the yeasty, breadiness of naan.

Most of her resupply stops only offered flatbread, but she'd hit the jackpot in Bennington. The owner of the hostel where she'd stayed had recommended Hannaford as the best grocery store option for the kinds of foods she preferred. Lucy had not been disappointed. In addition to the almond butter and naan, she pulled out a block of hard cheese. It was another luxury she didn't often find when her resupply was limited to Dollar General. She used the neck knife that hung between her breasts in a sheath strung like a necklace to slice off several pieces, then cleaned her knife, and returned the remaining cheese to its baggie.

Just then, she heard rustling and a clearly human tune being whistled. It was coming from the southern direction of the trail. For just a split second, her hope flared thinking Jacks may have already caught up to her, but no, it was just another random hiker. Based on how skinny he was, Lucy figured he was likely a thru-hiker. Men seemed to struggle to maintain weight while long distance hiking. Where Lucy was excited to find her clothes fitting a bit looser, she often heard her male counterparts complaining about bony knees and not enough padding on their hips.

Lucy bobbed her head at him and stuck a slice of cheese in her mouth while she massaged the almond butter to mix the oil back into it.

"Mind if I join you?" he asked her.

Lucy offered him a polite smile and said, "Sure."

Then she ignored him and chomped another slice of cheese while spreading her almond butter on the naan.

When she looked up again, she found him staring at her and sitting directly on the ground. It struck her as odd, but then "normal" people were rarely found hiking more than two thousand miles along the spine of the Appalachian Mountains. On-trail, "normal" was a relative term that often paired with body odor, peculiar eating habits, and a shovel to dig a hole when one needed to shit in the middle of the woods.

"You headed north or south?" he asked her.

She pretended to misunderstand his question and offered the same evasive answer she usually gave by simply replying, "Oh, I'm planning to do the whole trail eventually, but some of it I go north and some I hike south." It wasn't a lie. She was hiking northbound through the northern half of the trail before picking back up in Harpers Ferry and hiking south to Georgia.

He hummed at her before asking, "How far you going on this trip?"

She noticed that he'd set his pack down beside himself but hadn't opened it. He also didn't have any trekking poles. While not all hikers used them, they were often a topic of heated discussion and made a great diversion from questions she didn't really feel comfortable answering.

"You don't use trekking poles, huh?"

"What?" He looked confused.

Lucy's brow furrowed, and she wished the almond butter and naan didn't stick in her mouth so much. Normally, she liked that it encouraged her to eat slowly and enjoy her food, but right then, she wanted to be done and on her way. While she chewed, she bobbed her head toward her own poles and debated how she could grab her stuff and finish her dinner while making progress along the trail.

"Oh, you mean hiking poles," he seemed to have understood her nod and figured out what she was asking about. "Nah, having grown up in the woods, I don't see no point in leaning on sticks when I can walk along just fine."

Lucy had met all kinds of people along the trail. There were businessmen, housewives, retired people, down-on-their luck individuals with nothing better to do and nowhere better to be, and lots of recent college graduates looking to explore before settling down with a regular job. This guy, however, reminded her more of the country boys back home than anyone she'd met along the trail before. Yes, he was comfortable in the woods, but that was the thing: he seemed almost TOO comfortable.

"Are you local?" she asked without thinking.

He held out his hand, "My name's Frank. It's nice to meet you."

No way was that a trail name. He might just be too new to the trail to have earned one, or he might have chosen not to take one and just always use his real name, but...

"I'm Loner. I'm not known for being the most friendly or social. In fact, I probably ought to get going before the sun starts to set on me." She balanced what was left of her naan on her leg while reclosing the top of her canister and clasping the closures of her pack. Then she took another bite and balanced it on her pack while rolling up her sit pad.

Frank wasn't done, though, "You have any adventures today?" He was looking at her, not her face. It was like he was studying her response.

"It's funny you ask about that," she responded pointedly. Then she smiled, faked a laugh, and finished, "I'm easily freaked out by the woods and scared the crap out of myself earlier when a squirrel had wandered nearby." Frank was not a normal hiker, and it was time for Lucy to go.

She stuffed the last of her dinner into her mouth, hoisted her pack on her back and slid the straps of her poles over her hands and onto her wrists. She hated that he'd see the direction she was hiking in, but there was no way around it. The trail only ran north and south. She'd seen surprisingly few hikers today. She was ahead of the "bubble" of thru hikers who all departed Georgia in March and April. She'd never really found the trail empty before, so she was hopeful there would be others at the shelter when she arrived to make camp.

She briefly considered hiking south instead of north to bump into Jacks again sooner. Even though she knew his real name, she couldn't help but think of him as Jacks. But that would mean running for help and giving up on her quest, and she wasn't willing to do that, not even for one night. After the accident, there had been a moment when she'd looked around and realized how much of her life had curved and bent to align with Ben's. The same had certainly been true for him, but she was the one left standing here on earth trying to figure out what to do now that he was gone. And she had quickly realized that step one was to become herself again. Herself as an individual and not half of a whole.

That's how her adventures had begun. She'd packed up the house, thrown everything in storage, hired a property manager to rent the place out, and gone on a journey to find herself. The most important rediscovery had come while camping. She was an outdoorswoman. Sure, they'd hiked and camped while married, but the responsibilities and adventures had both been shared equally between the two of them. Now she knew that not only could she handle it all herself, but the challenge of doing so breathed life into her soul.

Since then, almost all her adventures had been outdoor explorations. She'd hiked through Zion and Glacier National Parks and wandered between giant redwood trees. She had found herself. Hiking the Appalachian Trail felt like her graduation ceremony. There was nothing left to prove; no hidden truths left to reveal. This adventure was her celebration of her rediscovered strength. It would take a whole lot more than a small cache of weapons and one creepy dude to change her course.

So, she continued her northbound hike.

Chapter 3

JACKS

He had enjoyed watching Lucy's ass as she walked away from him up the trail. Hikers had the best butts, and hers was especially attractive. Even before she'd revealed her real name, he couldn't think of her as "Loner." He could picture her sometimes feeling a bit "lonely," but her smile was much too bright for her to truly prefer only the company of herself.

As Jacks covered his last southbound mile, he couldn't help comparing her to the other women he'd met on the trail over the last decade. Most of them had been young and eager for excitement and drama. He'd had many try to snuggle up with him or latch on with an interest in sharing his tent, but that had never been why he'd hiked the trail. That first time he'd stumbled onto the footpath, he'd been young and thought he was looking for exactly that kind of thing. Once he'd entered the green tunnel, though, he'd realized this trail was his heaven.

When the soles of his trail runners hit the dirt between white blazes, he found a peace he'd never known existed. He'd always remember his first night in the woods. Several of the people he'd come with had been freaked out by the sounds and shadows found in the forest, but not Jacks. They'd called to each other to check in and reassure themselves that all was well. Jacks had been forced to stifle his urge to shush them so that he could enjoy the night.

By the time he'd hit Neel Gap, just about thirty miles into the trail, all but one of his friends had decided they'd had enough. Jacks had decided he wanted to live on the trail. While he'd had to jump off about a week later because of his grandmother, his final companion had made it all the way to Maine that year. Collin continued to give Jacks advice and had joined him for a few sections over the years.

The memory of that phone call still hit him sometimes, usually when he was alone on the trail like this. He'd been somewhere in North Carolina, maybe a week past Neel Gap, finally hitting his stride. The rhythm of walking, eating, sleeping had become as natural as breathing. He'd felt like he could walk forever.

Then his phone had buzzed with a call from a number he didn't recognize. He almost didn't answer it.

"Logan? Honey, it's Mrs. Patterson from next door to your grandmother."

His stomach had dropped before she'd even finished the sentence. Nana never asked the neighbors to call for her. She was too proud, too independent.

"She's in the hospital, sweetheart. She didn't want to worry you, but she collapsed yesterday morning. The doctors... well, they think you should come."

He'd stood there on the trail, pack still on his back, staring at the white blazes ahead of him disappearing into the green tunnel. This was supposed to be his time. His adventure. His chance to prove he could do something big and meaningful on his own.

But even as those thoughts ran through his head, he was already calculating how quickly he could get to a road, find a ride to the nearest bus station.

When he'd finally made it to the hospital two days later, Nana had been sitting up in bed, looking smaller and frailer than he'd ever seen her, but her eyes had lit up when he walked in.

"Logan, honey, you didn't have to come. I know how important that trail is to you."

"The trail will always be there, Nana," he'd said, surprising himself with how easily the words came. "But you won't. And you're more important."

She'd reached for his hand with fingers that felt like paper. "Logan, honey, the trail will always be there. But the people who love you? We're only here for a little while. Real strength isn't proving you can do something alone, it's knowing when something else matters more."

Those words had stayed with him through her final weeks, through the funeral, through the years since. They'd shaped how he approached relationships, how he understood the difference between independence and isolation. They'd taught him that the strongest people weren't the ones who never needed anyone else, they were the ones who knew when to put someone else's needs alongside their own.

Maybe that's why Lucy felt different to him. She wasn't hiking alone because she was running from connection, she was hiking alone because she'd already learned how to be herself. She'd chosen solitude from a place of strength, not fear.

As Jacks had grown up, he'd found himself congregating with a different variety of hikers. He no longer hesitated to hush the young adventurers and preferred swapping stories with the retired folks who had a lifetime of tales and wisdom to share. Those women were strong and fierce and fought for each of their accomplishments. It made him realize that was what he hoped to someday find. He wanted a woman who was with him because they wanted him, not because they needed him.

Sometimes he found himself with people in their thirties and forties like himself. He often enjoyed the company of those men, even if they got a bit too competitive for his taste. The women were a different story. He'd met one a few years ago who went by the name "Extra," and it had been the perfect name for her. She was recently divorced and "finding herself" again. For her that meant extra-long diatribes about how she was taking charge of her own life, right before she climbed into the tent of a male hiker. She alternated between mourning the end of her marriage and bragging about not having to set up her own tent in more than three hundred miles. That seemed to be the theme for many of the middle-aged women he met; they were all a bit lost and looking to find something along the trail.

Lucy had seemed different. As they ate and she talked about her husband, Jacks had seen how much she missed him, but she smiled when she talked about him. Her memories felt like cherished treasures that made her happy instead of bitter anguish or sad mourning. The more he contemplated his memories, the more confident he was that his impressions were supported by her six hundred solo miles with no tramily. That kind of self-sufficiency was impressive. Sure, anyone could hike by themselves, Jacks did it all the time, but the true test of the trail was mental.

Just like his old hiking buddies who freaked themselves out in the dark forest that first night, most hikers battled their own minds more than anything else. Long distance hiking was monotonous. As much as each section of the trail was unique, the reality was that a dirt path between the trees looks like a dirt path between the trees day after day. The climbs were brutal, but the downhills were painful on the knees. The rain and snow and wind and heat all made every day challenging.

For Lucy to have plodded along through all of that for almost two months with only her own mental fortitude left Jacks in awe. He was excited to meet up with her again.

There was no way he could catch her that night, but he wasn't about to lollygag around, either. He arrived back at Melville Neuheim Shelter in time for an early dinner. He'd love to continue, but stealth-camping was banned through this section of trail. The next permitted site was more than eight miles away. If it was a full moon, he might go ahead and hike into the night, but this was the new moon, and darkness in the forest was complete.

As he sprawled in his tent with his feet propped up on his backpack, he thought about all the things he wanted to tell Lucy and wondered if she'd be willing to stay in touch back in civilization.

By the time the sun rose, he was packed up, fed, and headed up the trail. Maybe he could catch her at lunch.

LUCY

Lucy arrived at Goddard Shelter with two fingers of space between the bottom of the sun and the tops of the trees. That gave her about thirty minutes before the sunlight would dim. Her shin had acted up again those last few miles, and she'd wished she'd been able to stretch and massage it more at her dinner break. After her encounter with Frank, she'd been hiking faster than she should have and hadn't taken many breaks. The upside was her early arrival in camp. It was nice to be setting up her tent by the light of the setting sun instead of her headlamp.

After leaning her pack against the shelter, she made her way down to the spring and began looking for a spot to set up her tent. She was happy to be the first to arrive since there weren't many tent spots by this shelter. Unfortunately, it also meant she was alone. Hopefully other hikers would be arriving.

Lucy went about getting her tent set up, her sleeping pad inflated, and her things arranged the way she liked. She wiped away the sweat of the day and changed into clean, dry camp clothes. She was starting to think this might be a solo night at camp when she heard the rhythmic rustle and chatter of new arrivals.

When they emerged from the trees, she was relieved to see that it was a couple who appeared completely unconnected to Frank. The man had a normal Gregory pack, the woman was wearing Hoka trail running shoes, and they both carried trekking poles.

"Good evening," she called out to them.

"Oh, hello! Not too many people out here today. We were starting to wonder if we'd have the place to ourselves tonight," the woman called back with a grin. "I'm Grasshopper, and this is Tag-a-long." She gestured to the man walking just behind her.

"I'm Loner. Nice to meet you." The standard trail introductions reassured Lucy that she was back on familiar ground. "How far'd you go today?" she asked them as they peeled off their packs and stretched their shoulders.

"Meh, not too far, just up from the other shelter," Tag-a-long replied while Grasshopper gave him the side-eye.

Lucy chuckled at the vague answer that matched so many of her own. "I'm NoBo. You?" She hoped that if she shared her northbound direction, they'd be more willing to open up. Between the unsettling quiet of Hell Hollow, the odd shadow creature she may or may not have spotted, and her creepy encounter with Frank, Lucy was feeling uncomfortable on the trail for the first time. For once, she didn't want to live up to her "Loner" trail name.

"Oh yeah, we're just doing a small section," Grasshopper commented before telling Tag-a-long to go refill their water. "How's your hike been?" she asked.

This was the perfect opening, "Actually," Lucy started, "I had an odd run-in with a guy when I stopped for dinner. He didn't seem like a normal hiker and kinda weirded me out. Honestly, I'm glad you two showed up tonight. I normally love camping solo, but…" Lucy shrugged and felt stupid for sounding so uncertain and insecure.

"Yeah, I understand that! You're out here by yourself?" Grasshopper looked concerned.

"I usually prefer my own company, hence the name, but today has been unusual. I don't suppose you came up from the south?" Lucy figured they had to SoBo since she hadn't seen them at all before. It was possible that they'd been behind her all day, though. If that was the case, she was eager to find out if they'd run into Frank or experienced anything else odd.

"Oh, no, um, we're heading that way tomorrow." Grasshopper looked uncomfortable. She bent over her pack as she answered and began digging around.

Lucy watched and thought. Something felt off, but she couldn't figure out what.

Tag-a-long returned with their water and asked Grasshopper what she was doing. The two went back and forth discussing what was packed where and how to set things up. Eventually, they'd picked an area up against Lucy's space. There was barely room to walk between the tents, though Lucy wasn't confident Grasshopper and Tag-a-long's tent would ever actually stand. Each time they placed one pole, another popped free. It was obvious Grasshopper was becoming frustrated and Tag-a-long was enjoying the entertainment.

At first it annoyed Lucy to have them so close, but after the third time a pole popped free, she couldn't help laughing just a bit. When they still didn't have the tent up ten minutes later, Lucy's bemusement had shifted into disbelief. How were these two both experienced enough to have trail names, but inexperienced enough to struggle setting up their tent?

For just a second, Lucy considered packing up and hiking on. Generally, when her spidey-senses spoke to her, she listened. But she was smart enough to evaluate risk in a rational way. The sun was setting, her leg was hurting, there was no moon, and she was tired. Hiking on was a guaranteed danger; these two were more likely to end up turning into a funny story she could tell Jacks about tomorrow.

"Would you like an extra hand?" Lucy volunteered. Sometimes turning strangers into friends really was the best approach.

"Yes. Please. That would be amazing." Grasshopper blew away the strands of hair that had escaped her ponytail as she looked up with both gratitude and desperation.

"Here. I'll get this end, and you get that end." Lucy held two of the poles in place while Grasshopper set the other two, and then the tent was up.

"Thank you." Grasshopper said clearly relieved. "How do you do it by yourself?"

"You learn. Once you get used to it, it's not so hard," Lucy assured her.

"And you're totally comfortable out here on your own? I mean, don't you worry about safety or anything?" Apparently, Grasshopper noticed Lucy's frustration with the question because she quickly hurried on, "I mean, like I always learned that you should hike in pairs. Do you have someone you stay in touch with or check in or use a GPS tracker or something?"

Tag-a-long had quit laughing and was intently listening to the conversation now.

Were these two normal weird or concerning weird? When in doubt, Lucy always decided to err on the side of caution, "Oh yeah, I have a GPS tracker and check in with a couple people regularly. If I miss a check in or my tracker moves or doesn't move as expected, they alert the authorities right away. In fact, I'm due for a check in later tonight." She did, in fact, have a Garmin InReach with her, but the only people she messaged on it were her parents. They wouldn't become alarmed until they hadn't heard from her for forty-eight hours. Even with the satellite and GPS, connections on the AT just weren't that reliable.

She gathered up all her things and climbed inside her tent. As she relaxed, she listened in on Grasshopper and Tag-a-long instead of listening to her normal audiobook or music. The two of them bantered, teased, and argued over sleeping arrangements. It felt normal. She didn't hear either of them plotting her death, discussing automatic weapons, or making any other evil plans.

Lucy was starting to question her own sanity. In her experience, that meant it was time for bed. She snuggled in and drifted off. Tomorrow would be a new day.

Chapter 4

JACKS

By eight am Jacks was already crossing the footbridge at Hell Hollow. He was enjoying listening to the birds chirping and a playful squirrel was running back and forth alongside him. It would dart forward to scout ahead and then run back, chirp, rustle, and run ahead again.

The heat hadn't crept into the day yet, so Jacks was able to move quickly and didn't often need to refill his water. He planned to stop at Goddard Shelter for a refill and a quick bite to eat. Until then, he was enjoying the snacks he kept handy while climbing up toward Little Pond Mountain.

The squirrel met up with a friend, and Jacks watched the two of them clamber off through the ferns and back toward some beautiful purple flowers standing tall between the trees. Jacks considered going to pick one for Lucy, but that would violate his Leave No Trace principles, so he didn't. Instead, he took just a moment to veer off the trail far enough to be able to get a nice picture of one of the flowers. It looked like a poppy, but those were usually red. These were a very bright purple.

Jacks managed to arrive at the side trail toward Goddard Shelter by eleven am. He knew Lucy would have already packed up and left for the day. He debated just hiking on by to catch up with her sooner, but the sun was rising high, and he could use more water. The spring by the shelter was really the only water source in this eleven-mile stretch of trail. He turned to follow the blue blazes.

LUCY

Lucy started to toss and turn because she was chilly, so she tried to snuggle deeper into her sleeping bag. When she reached out for it, everything her hand touched was damp. This was not good, but she wasn't sure exactly what the problem was. She fought to wake up enough to figure out why she was wet. She rolled over and flopped her hand around beside her, then jolted awake when there was no crinkle of her sleeping pad, and her hand encountered leaves, dirt, and rocks instead of the bottom of her tent.

Her vision was a bit fuzzy, and her head was throbbing, but she was alert enough now to realize that she was lying on bare ground with no mat, no tent, no bag, covered in dew, and with leaves stuck in her hair.

Lucy was usually a morning person. Waking up groggy to find the sun already completely above the horizon was unnerving. She felt a hot flash of pain shoot through her left wrist when she leaned on it to sit up, so she used her right arm instead. She took just a second to catalog the rest of her body parts and found a few scratches and scrapes along with sore spots she expected to eventually blossom into bruises, but no other serious injuries. Both her ankles could comfortably roll in circles. She could pull her knees up to her chest and straighten them again without discomfort. Her right arm was supporting her upper body without complaint.

She looked around to get her bearings and found no shelter in sight. With a deep breath in, Lucy forced herself not to panic and take a moment to assess the situation. Long ago, she'd learned how to handle getting lost in the woods. Her knack for going missing had allowed her entire Girl Scout troop to earn their Search and Rescue badges when she was a kid. As she exhaled, she settled into what she knew she needed to do: S.T.O.P. The "S" reminded her to sit still; "T" meant think about what you know; "O" stood for observe where you are, what you have, and what's around you; "P" was plan your next steps.

Normally, this method resulted in Lucy hugging a tree and singing while waiting for someone to find her, but this wasn't normal. The only way one wakes up in an unknown location with nothing but the clothes on their back is if they've been partying too hard or have been drugged. Lucy clearly remembered crawling into her tent completely sober the night before, so she knew she fell into the second category. It was time to think and think hard! She had no idea how she'd gotten here, where "here" was, or who had moved her from the comfort of her tent. Her first thoughts went to Frank, but she'd put some distance between them. Besides, Grasshopper and Tag-a-long totally would have heard something happening, unless they were involved. Could Frank just be your average weirdo while Grasshopper and Tag-a-long were the real problem?

What did she know about them? They were clearly comfortable hiking but unfamiliar with setting up a tent. They knew to filter their water but hadn't seemed to know each other's strengths and weaknesses when camping. It was obvious that they were well acquainted, but in hindsight, Lucy thought the situation had been unfamiliar to them. This suggested day hikers who didn't do overnights. That probably meant locals, maybe.

Ok, time for observation. What resources did she have? Lucy clutched her chest and was excited to realize she still had her neck knife! The knife itself was much less useful than many people liked to think, but it was something, and the paracord it hung from could prove useful in several different situations. She also had her clothes, which wasn't anything to sneeze at. She had on her wool underwear and black sports bra. She was wearing her wool leggings that she used as camp pants and sleep pants. The best news was her shirt, though. In addition to her gray base layer, she also had on her blaze orange technical T-shirt. It was made of polyester, not cotton, and fit her very loosely. She had thrown it on over her base layer last night as the temperatures dropped after sunset.

Lucy was far from feeling okay with the situation, but she was starting to calm down. She continued her observation. She was still wearing the wool socks she slept in, but now her trail runner shoes were on her feet. Her brow furrowed in confusion. She had not worn her shoes to bed. She never even brought her shoes inside her tent. She always kept them in the vestibule under the rain cover but on bare ground so as not to track debris into her sleep space. Why on Earth would whoever drugged and moved her have put her shoes on but not removed her blaze orange shirt?

Another deep breath had Lucy prioritizing. She could think about the "whys" of things later. Right now, she needed to plan. While she was chilly, the sun was up, and the temperature was climbing. Her wool clothing provided insulation even when damp. Assuming that whoever dragged her out here was a local, she didn't think calling out or waiting for rescue was a reasonable option. While she knew she could survive a long time without food, her need for water was much more immediate. She needed to self-rescue.

She thought back on what she knew. Downhill led to water and water led to civilization. On the other hand, climbing burned energy quickly. Also, it often left one stranded on a ridge with no water or shelter. The Appalachian trail ran along the ridge. She'd hiked downhill toward the shelter, so the trail was likely uphill. She had no idea if she was east or west of the trail. Then the scariest thought occurred to her: What if they had driven her far, far away? All her previous thinking assumed that she was still in southern Vermont and somewhere in the vicinity of the AT and the Vermont Long Trail.

Crying wastes water, and she didn't have any to spare. She sucked in another breath and blew it out fiercely. She could do this. She would do this. And then she would find and fuck up the assholes who'd put her in this position. Lucy took another moment to be grateful for having spent the last year and a half rebuilding her sense of self, then she checked the forest floor around her hoping to find something, anything, that had been dropped or left behind. She came up empty.

She was going to hike downhill. She was not going to second-guess herself. She was going to move at a reasonable speed until she found water or a dry creek bed. That would be her guiding light. Her shin felt tight, so Lucy stretched and used her right hand to massage it just like Jacks had said. She was sure he'd be looking for her, but he'd be looking in the wrong place. As far as he knew, she was still north of him on the trail, and he'd keep hurrying along hoping to catch up with her.

Lucy made one last decision before setting off. Her blaze orange shirt was important, but she wasn't sure how. She could shred it to make flags and leave a trail. This would enable her to tell if she doubled back on herself and would give any search and rescue who came looking a trail to follow. It would also provide whoever left her out here with a trail to follow. If she continued to wear it, the orange shirt would make her clearly visible in the forest, allowing both rescuers and pursuers to spot her more easily. There were pros and cons to both options, but in the end, she decided to shred it.

If the bad guys wanted to come and get her, they likely already knew where to find her. If they spotted her out moving through the woods and realized she was not only alive but moving, there was a greater chance they'd decide to kill her. She was hedging her bets that her trail of thin orange flags would go unnoticed. Plus, she could use a strip of it to tie a sling to support her left wrist.

By the time Lucy figured out how to hold her shirt between her feet and teeth while using her knife to cut it into strips, the day had warmed, and her wrist had developed a steady throb even when tucked carefully against her side.

JACKS

When Jacks arrived at the end of the blue-blazed side trail, he was surprised to spot a tent standing nearby. The tent looked to be in good condition, not abandoned. Midday was the least likely time to find a tent fully set up unless a hiker was hurt or sick. This was the time that they were all out on the trail, and even if they stopped for lunch and/or a nap, no one ever dug out and set up their tent for that.

Jacks flashed back to Lucy flinching and wincing in pain from shin splints and rushed toward the tent with visions of her lying inside, too injured to continue hiking. "Knock-knock," he said quietly so as not to scare her. He got no response.

He unzipped the flap and peeked inside to find only Lucy's pack, and it was clearly Lucy's pack. As she'd walked away from him the previous day, he'd noticed the "All Women, All Trails" patch on the back of her gray Osprey. It was the same patch and pack he was looking at now.

He rezipped the tent and stepped back to think. Could she just be using the privy?

Jacks looked around to find the trail that would lead to the pit or composting toilet provided for hikers camping at the shelter and heard a shout that directed his attention. It wasn't a scream or a call for help, but more a grunt of frustration. Thinking that it was Lucy and that he could help, he headed that direction. Sure enough, the sound had come from the privy trail. He could hear quiet voices now but couldn't tell what they were discussing. He slowed his steps as his brow furrowed. The voices were too deep to be Lucy.

Just then there was another loud huff and the sounds of someone coming his direction. Before he could make any conscious decisions about what to do, a tall, skinny man appeared in front of him. He looked like your average, bony thru-hiker, so Jacks breathed out and reminded himself to think first and act second. This guy could likely tell him where Lucy was.

"Hi, have you been here long? I'm trying to catch up with a friend." Jacks kept his stance relaxed and tried to appear unconcerned.

The thru-hiker just grunted at him and pushed past.

Jacks turned to follow him back to the shelter and decided to try a different approach. "Who were you talking to back there? I don't suppose it was a woman?" Maybe it had been Lucy and she'd been on her way to the privy.

The hiker studied him for a second before replying, "It was another guy here to use the outhouse."

Every hair on Jacks' body stood to full attention. This was WRONG! In all his time on the trail, not once had he ever heard the word outhouse. The signs all said "privy" because that's what they were called. Outhouses were bathrooms found out behind houses; privies were where hikers went to deposit their business. Jacks had been wrong. This man was not a thru-hiker.

"Oh, is that his stuff?" Jacks asked innocently while pointing to Lucy's tent.

The guy squinted his eyes at Jacks and took a few steps toward him while sticking his hand in his pocket, and Jacks' internal alarm bells fell into the background as his brain began screaming at him, time to run away now!

"Why, the fuck, are you so nosy?" the not-a-hiker asked.

Jacks heard the crack of a snapped branch behind him just before he was pushed forward and a young, male voice said, "Kick his ass, Frank!"

Well, Jacks thought, at least now I know this guy's name is Frank, and the guy behind me is too chickenshit to do anything himself. Then he curled his hands around both of his trekking poles and began swinging them like a baseball bat with every ounce of strength that he had.

Sure enough, Frank pulled a knife from his pocket, flipped it open and began swinging and stabbing in return. Chickenshit continued to taunt them both but stayed far enough back to keep out of the fight. As they circled each other, swinging and grunting, Jacks managed to get in a few good hits to Frank's head. Frank managed to swing his knife past Jacks' thigh at one point, but it was a glancing slice and not a serious stab wound.

Just as Jacks could tell Frank was getting tired (and Jacks was thanking the universe for his own physical conditioning), a loud female roared, "Enough!"

It fully caught Frank's attention, which allowed Jacks to take off sprinting into the brush between Frank and Chickenshit. He could hear the other three chasing him as he leapt logs, ducked under branches, and ripped his way through thorny bushes. Jacks was paying no attention to the direction he was going. His only focus was on getting away.

Eventually, his foot caught a rock wrong, and he tumbled and rolled down through leaves and dirt until he managed to grab a tiny tree and flop himself into a sitting position. As soon as he stilled, he listened with everything he had, fully expecting to hear the chase continuing behind him. Instead, he heard nothing but silence. Apparently, his flight had shocked even the squirrels and birds into silence.

He sat and listened and thought until the normal forest noises resumed. Then he took stock of his situation. The pocket he kept his phone in had fallen victim to Frank's crazy knife swiping, but the cut on his leg appeared to be minor. He'd once been scratched worse by an angry cat. Everything on his phone was backed up to the cloud, so it wouldn't be too hard to replace. Though it did mean that he didn't have any way to call for help. Nor did he have GPS to guide him back to the AT. Looking around, he figured that if he climbed uphill, he could probably get back up to the trail.

Before standing, he took a moment to pull off his pack and check that it was okay. He removed the straps of his trekking poles from his wrists and noted that both poles had snapped during his escape. It meant he'd have to find branches or something to hold up his tent, but he could replace his poles the next time he was in town. He no longer had the closed-cell foam pad he used as a sit pad and kept strapped to the outside of his pack. Much like the loss of his trekking poles, it would make his journey less comfortable but didn't pose any serious concerns. One of the Crocs he kept clipped to his pack for around camp and wading across streams was also missing. Everything else appeared to be fine.

Jacks left the handles of his poles lying in the leaves and began trudging uphill but away from where he'd tumbled down. Since it was midday, the sun was almost directly overhead. Jacks wasn't sure if he was heading east or west, but he remembered the shelter was on west side of the trail and he'd been a bit up the trail to the privy, so he figured he was probably headed east and back toward the AT. Climbing up without a path to follow was tough work, but he was in good shape. He didn't go straight up, but sideways and up to avoid ending up right back at the shelter with Frank and the gang.

Jacks knew it would take longer to return to the trail with his roundabout path, and it bugged him that he couldn't check his progress on his phone. Everything had happened before he'd had a chance to refill his water, so after an hour of bushwhacking with no discernible progress, worry started to creep into the back of his mind. He kept reminding himself, "I am fit and brave and experienced." He just needed to trust himself and keep going.

A few minutes later, Jacks noticed an orange ribbon tied around a branch. He'd seen something like this many times before. People who owned private land along the trail often used them to mark their property. When he took the time to look around, he soon spotted a matching strip farther away.

Normally, he was respectful enough to stay off private property, but there was officially nothing normal about this trip. If he followed the property line, it was likely to lead to a road, driveway, or at least a corner.

Even though it meant shifting to walking downhill instead of up, Jacks decided to follow the orange markers.

Chapter 5

LUCY

Lucy was running out of shirt. The general rule of thumb was the next marker should be placed just before the last marker disappeared. This created two points that could be used to create a line to follow. Stop at one marker, look around until the next is found, walk to it, and repeat. Unfortunately, about half her shirt had been used to make her sling. She'd sliced the rest of it into the thinnest and shortest strips she could expect to still be reasonably visible, but there was only so much material. She had yet to find water or even a dry creek bed to follow. Her pace had slowed as she tried to figure out what to do once she ran out of markers.

Just as the day started to feel truly hot and thirst began to plague her, she heard someone following her. Her first instinct was to run, but she stifled it and sat down next to a tree instead. She knew herself well enough to know that this panic would cause her to wander in crazy directions. It would make her situation worse instead of better. With a little luck, she could hide in the brush until they passed, and then continue on her way. Whoever it was walked quickly and without stopping.

She hunkered down behind a large fallen log and crossed her fingers. The sounds and the person came closer and closer. She stopped breathing when the footsteps stopped just on the other side of the log. In her head, Lucy was silently chanting, "Maybe it's a bear. Please, let it be a bear." Then she rolled her eyes at herself and considered just how messed up it was that she was hoping to encounter a bear instead of a human. Man, this hike had gone sideways on her.

Just as Lucy was about to bang her head on a nearby rock in frustration, aggravation, and self-disgust, someone or something touched her shoulder. That was the end of calm and logical Lucy.

She leapt from her spot while screaming and wailing, grabbing the nearby rock and swinging it around as she tried to figure out which direction to throw it. With her feet spread wide, she prepared to crotch-kick whoever had dared to touch her. This might be the end, but she would not go down without a fight! Sliding her left arm from the sling, she planned to scratch her nails as deep as possible into her attacker's flesh. At least then evidence would point to who to prosecute when someone eventually found her body.

"Whoa, whoa, easy, Lucy, it's me. It's okay. It's just me, Logan, "Jacks," whatever you want to call me. I didn't mean to scare you." Jacks was huddled on the forest floor with his pack still on his back.

"Holy shit! What in the hell are you doing here?" She shouted at him while bringing her volume back under control and dropping her rock back to the forest floor. "How did you find me? Oh, thank God, we're still in Vermont!" Lucy resettled her left arm in her makeshift sling and began to pace around the area while muttering to herself.

"Lucy!"

"Huh? Oh, sorry," she forced both her feet and mind to stop spinning and focused on Jacks. Once he had her attention, he looked a bit sheepish and began rubbing the back of his neck and scuffing his toes in the dirt. "Seriously," she prompted him, "how did you end up here?"

"Well, the short answer is that I'm apparently following the same property line that you are," he shrugged as he replied.

Lucy's brow furrowed in confusion until Jacks bobbed his head at one of the orange strips she'd tied nearby.

"Landowners mark their property line by tying ribbons around trees. It's common around here. I think the colors might sometimes mean something, but to be honest, I never paid that much attention. I'm kind of regretting that now." Jacks stared off into the distance, brows furrowed, as he rambled.

Lucy tried to stifle her laugh, but a tiny giggle may have leaked out causing Jacks to look at her questioningly. She lifted the arm in the blaze orange sling made from the same t-shirt as her ripped up tree markers and explained to him what she'd been doing.

"Oh, I guess I wasn't following a property line after all, huh?" The way he grinned at her with crinkles around the corners of his eyes made it obvious that he felt both chagrined to have been called out, but also appreciative of her knowledge and work. "I guess that means we're still lost." His expression grew more serious at that acknowledgement.

"Well," Lucy said, "Yes and no. There's lots of good news for me. I've been worried that I might not even be in Vermont anymore, and that's been settled. I also didn't have anything in the way of supplies, but I see you have your pack at least. So again, that's an improvement on my situation, but you still haven't told me what happened to you."

Jacks sighed, "It's a bit of a story, and I don't know about you, but I could use more water. Any chance you've found a stream or anything?"

"You have no idea how excited I am to hear that you still have your water filter. I mean, it typically takes three days before waterborne illnesses take a person down, and I figured I should be able to find someone by then. But I'd much rather avoid the issue altogether. I haven't hit water yet, but that's the direction I'm heading. Once we find something, we'll sit and drink and catch up on our adventures."

"Wait, if you're lost, how do you know you're heading toward water?" Jacks asked as Lucy started off again continuing her downhill path.

He followed her as she explained to him over her shoulder, "We're in the mountains, where the watershed begins. All the springs and tiny streams along the trail are headwaters and tributaries that lead down to larger waterways. Since all water flows downhill, if we hike downhill, it's very likely we'll hit a waterway. Based on the way there's a ridge in front of us, a ridge behind us, and knobby-looking hill to our right, I'm guessing we'll find a small stream down where the three slopes collide."

"Okaaaaay," Jacks dragged out the word, and Lucy braced herself for an obnoxious comment or response. "I think you officially know much more about the woods than me. So, you lead the way, and I'll carry the pack. Oh, but when we stop, I want to look at your arm. Would you rather I did that now?"

Lucy might have fallen in love with him right in that moment, but if he was also out of water, they needed to move. Dehydration was their most immediate threat. Everything else could wait.

JACKS

They continued to bushwhack their way along. Lucy was moving a little slower than Jacks would prefer, but she was injured and the first one to fight through the underbrush while maintaining her sense of direction. He certainly was not about to voice any complaints about anything. He offered her the last of his water, and she gladly accepted it. As much as discovering her well-founded plan and competence relieved him, he regretted that he couldn't do more to help her.

After she'd pointed out the terrain to him, he could clearly see where a hill on their right connected the two ridges in front of and behind them. The ground continued its downhill slope to his left. Just about the time he thought they'd have to veer left to continue downhill, Lucy stopped. She did that often to look around and keep herself oriented, or so he assumed, but this pause seemed a bit different. He realized that she was looking down instead of up, the way she had before.

Then she did turn left and set off at a quicker pace. After just a few yards, she stopped again and turned back to him. "I think I found water, but I need your help."

Her wish was his command. He smiled as he made his way over to her. "Just tell me what to do."

"See those rocks?" she asked him. Once he'd nodded, she continued, "If you look just past them, you can see where the leaves are wet. I'm betting that if we move aside some of the leaves, we'll find a spring buried in among the rocks. I can get over there, but I'm going to need a literal hand to move stuff around and find water that we can collect."

Jacks couldn't help looking at her and grinning. He'd met capable women before. He'd met smart women before. He'd even had some luck hitting on beautiful women before. But he wasn't sure he'd ever found all of that in the same woman.

He also wasn't about to let her further hurt her arm when he hadn't even managed to figure out what was wrong with it to start with.

"I have a better idea," he told her. "You sit with the pack over by this tree while I go dig around and find the water. It'll be easier for me without my pack on, and I'm guessing you've been without food or water for longer than me." She studied him for a second, so he added, "I know you finished off the last of my water, but that really wasn't much. I've seen how hard you've been working to find a path for us."

Her shoulders dropped as her breath escaped, and Jacks knew she'd agreed. He unbuckled all his straps, set down his backpack, and pulled out his Sawyer Squeeze. It was about the size of a toilet paper tube and was the same water filter that most hikers used. It kept life simple by attaching to any Smart Water bottle from any convenience store. He always carried two of the one-liter bottles with him, filling one with dirty water, attaching the filter, and squeezing the clean water into the second bottle.

For now, he handed the Sawyer to Lucy and grabbed his old bottle that was cut short to easily scoop water from smaller pools or puddles. Taking his dirty water bottle down to the rocks she'd pointed out, he had to dig around a bit more than expected. Lucy encouraged him to keep looking, and sure enough, when he moved one of the larger rocks, he found water pooling between the rocks below it. The pool wasn't big, but the water was crystal clear. He scooped it up until his bottle was full, then returned to Lucy to filter it.

Noticing how much she was licking her lips, he just handed her the bottle with the filter attached and told her to drink straight from the filter. The handy sports-like cap was designed for this exact purpose, and he didn't want her to have to wait any longer. His concern about her possible dehydration grew, especially since he didn't know how long she'd been lost out here without anything to drink.

Once she'd drunk her fill, he finished off that liter and went back to the spring for more. When he returned this time, he leaned the bottle against a nearby rock and asked to see Lucy's arm before they did anything else.

She obliged him and pulled it out of what he had to believe was an attempt at a makeshift sling. The improvised wrap didn't support her arm correctly at all, but it had kept it tucked against her chest. As soon as he saw it, he knew her wrist was broken. Swelling distorted it, and nasty shades of purple colored the skin. Normally, he would palpate the area to get a better idea of how and where the break was located, but that would hurt her, and he only had basic Ibuprofen for pain relief. He couldn't bring himself to cause her that much pain. Instead, Jacks settled for pulling out his spare base-layer top to make a proper support. The long-sleeved shirt offered compression by design, so he cut off one of the arms and helped her carefully slide her hand through.

Lucy's whimper nearly destroyed him, but he knew the improved support would help her in the long run. The much-improved arm brace supported her wrist, and he added a couple of straight sticks for additional stability. Then he told her that she must not use that arm for anything, under any circumstances. He would help her whenever she needed a second hand. She looked a bit doubtful, but the whole ordeal had also left her pale and trembling, so she didn't argue. He couldn't imagine how much worse the experience would be if he tried to poke and prod at the injury.

"Ok," she started a bit breathlessly, "no more avoiding it. Tell me about what happened." Then she leaned her head back against the tree trunk behind her and closed her eyes while breathing deeply.

Jacks figured his story would be a welcome distraction for her, so he started talking. He told her about spotting her tent by the shelter, his discussion with Frank, and the two other people he ended up running from. He explained the way he tripped and snapped his poles, along with his attempt to make it back to the trail before spotting her line of orange markings.

By the time he finished, color had returned to her face, and she was giving him a funny look. "What?" he asked.

Lucy shook herself, and he watched the disbelief disappear from her face. "Nothing. Sorry. I guess I'm just a bit surprised by your story."

Jacks considered pressing her for more, but she still hadn't eaten anything, it was now late afternoon, and they should both drink more water. He looked around for a minute.

"I know it's still early, but do you have any thoughts on where we should camp tonight?" The brush here was thick. Eventually, they'd need to find a spot to set up camp for the night. It would be much easier while they still had several hours of daylight left, so he didn't want to wait until dark to try and figure it out.

"If you're ok with it, I was thinking we should camp here tonight. We have water, we're going to have to clear a spot no matter where we go, and..." Lucy paused and sighed before continuing, "I'm really tired." She rolled the back of her head along the tree until she was looking over at him. She looked exhausted.

"Alright," Jacks said with determination. "Here's what we're going to do. First, we'll make some food and eat. We both need the energy. Then you tell me where, and I'll clear a spot for the tent." He grinned at her slyly. "After that, I'll interrogate you to learn the truth about how you ended up wandering through the woods with no gear." He stated the last bit in an artificial seriousness that made her huff out a laugh.

"Food sounds good. I hate to admit it, but I think it's been about twenty-four hours since I've eaten."

That was what Jacks figured, and he didn't like it. Her hand shook slightly the last couple times she'd taken a drink of water. For as long as he'd been hiking the trail, he never expected anything like this to happen, so he hadn't bothered to learn much about wilderness survival. Obviously, Lucy did not suffer the same arrogance. He was counting on her for things like choosing a direction and finding water, and he worried that she might be getting hungry beyond the point of being able to think clearly and make sound decisions.

Plus, he really missed the way she'd smiled, chatted, and laughed so freely during lunch the previous day. He wanted to see that spark reignite.

Chapter 6

Lucy didn't want to admit it to herself, let alone to Jacks, but she was struggling. As they'd hiked along, her legs started getting shaky, so she'd slowed her pace. By the time she'd spotted the wet leaves, she'd been focusing every ounce of strength she had left on just finding water. Jacks' offer to collect it himself had saved her. She had planned to try and get it herself, but was confident there would have been stumbling, struggling, and potential further injury during the process. When she'd first leaned back against the tree trunk, her head had swum, and instead of feeling better, she struggled not to pass out or throw up.

That first liter of water had helped her tremendously, but it didn't stop the shaking in her muscles. She needed food but wasn't sure how much Jacks had or if he'd be willing to share. As stupid as it sounded, Lucy did not like asking for help, even in situations like this.

When he stepped in and informed her of the plan, she felt a sense of relief she didn't know she needed. Finally, she was able to let her brain fuzz out and just focus on existing.

She'd barely blinked, and Jacks was handing her a pot of warm oatmeal.

"I added some cold water, so it shouldn't be too hot for you," he told her as she tried to grip the handle of the pot with her left hand. Instead of extending, it pulled on her shoulder, and pain slashed through her wrist. She couldn't hold both pot and spoon at the same time.

Luckily, Jacks noticed her looking around for a place to balance the pot. Based on the secure way he kept ahold of the pot, he anticipated her predicament, and maybe also been aware of how badly she was shaking. She reached with her right hand to pick up the spoon from where he'd set it on top of his pack, but he grabbed it before she could convince her muscles to follow her commands.

"Here. You relax. I'll handle holding stuff." He swooped the spoon through the oats and raised a small bite to her mouth.

Lucy wanted to be embarrassed. She wanted to turn red and insist she could do it herself. She was a capable, grown woman, and not someone who needed to be fed like a baby. She was also so tired she could barely keep her head up.

So, she said nothing and accepted the bite.

The first hit of sugar to her system made her woozy, forcing her to stop for a minute. Jacks didn't seem to mind though. He started chatting about one of his clients back in civilization who was trying to get back to hiking after having a knee replaced. It was an inconsequential buzz in the back of Lucy's mind, but it allowed her time without making her feel even more self-conscious.

Soon, the wooziness passed, and she was ready for a second bite. Jacks obliged her and continued his story. From there, things smoothed out a bit. Lucy's vision cleared causing her to wonder when it had gotten hazy and how she hadn't noticed. She felt steadier and more solid instead of wobbly like a Jello-mold trying to escape its form. By the time Jacks was scraping the edges of his pot, she was functioning well enough to realize that he was feeding her but not eating anything himself.

His story had wound down as her eating had picked up, so she didn't have to interrupt him to ask, "Aren't you having any?"

His face lit up, even though the smile he gave her was small. "I'll get myself something in just a minute. You kinda zoned out while I was cooking, and it had me a little worried. I'm glad you seem to be better now."

"Yeah, too much adventure; not enough food and water. Thank you. Seriously. I didn't notice just how bad I'd gotten."

"How are you feeling now? And please be honest with me." Jacks looked not really worried, but more concerned and like he wanted to help.

Lucy took a deep breath, stifled her urge to blow him off with assurances that she was fine, and took a moment to assess herself. No more dizziness; no more shaking; still tired; slight throb in her wrist; but overall, a big improvement.

"I'm a lot better than I was. Mostly thanks to you. I cannot say how glad I am that you kept your pack on while running." She gave him a teasing smile and was happy to see his face relax.

"Yeah, me too. Okay, where should I clear a spot for the tent?"

Lucy stood up slowly while Jacks hovered next to her. She didn't even mind his attention. With only one good wrist, she'd welcome his strength if she fell. The mere thought of landing on her wrist made her want to cry. On the other hand, the thought of landing on Jacks' chest made falling *almost* seem like a great idea. Oh yeah, she felt much better now.

She spotted a space between some trees that sat back away and uphill a bit from the spring. Ferns dominated the area with maybe a little bit of brush mixed in. She saw no thorny bushes, though, and the ground appeared as level as any other spot. She pointed it out to Jacks and started moving that way with slow steps that stretched her stiffening muscles.

Then she felt his hand on her shoulder blade as he said, "Whoa, let me go check it out. If there really aren't any thorns, and I think it's good, I'll come back and get you. This way you only have to go to the final spot and not wander all over as we scout all the options."

It had been a very long time since Lucy had the luxury of relaxing while someone else handled things. Part of her bristled at being encouraged to stay there, but the smart part of her was relieved to have a friend during this adventure. It would be good for her to have time to stretch anyway.

Sure enough, Jacks spent a few minutes looking around the area and pulling several small plants before returning to where she was standing near his pack.

"It looks pretty good. It's not totally level, and we need to move a bunch of rocks to smooth out the ground. Otherwise, I think that's our tent spot."

"Alright," Lucy started to pick up the pack, but Jacks grabbed it from her.

"I've got this. Save your energy for helping move rocks and try to smooth out the ground. I am happy to say that I do have a ZPacks Duplex, so the tent will be big enough for both of us. I only have one sleeping pad and one sleeping bag, though, so we should probably try to do something to insulate between the ground and the tent."

Lucy watched Jacks' eyebrows furrow with concentration as he thought through their arrangements for the night.

"And we'll need to find sticks to use in place of my trekking poles to support the tent."

Well, Lucy thought, *at least Jacks was aware of their hurdles.* She followed him up to the cleared spot while looking around for appropriate sticks. Her legs were done in, but after stretching she was convincing them to take one more step after another.

"Do you have extra paracord or rope for your bear bag or anything?" she asked him.

"Um, yeah, but don't we need the rope to hang our food? I have my wristband made of paracord, but that's all the extra I've got." He obviously didn't understand where she was going with this.

"That might be enough. If not, we can shorten the bear hang a little. No one ever camps here from the look of things, so I highly doubt we'll encounter any bears accustomed to getting food from humans. We can pull apart the paracord and tie the top corners of the tent to those two branches." Lucy pointed to branches on opposite sides of the clearing that were both just above Jacks' head height. Since Lucy's neck knife was also strung on paracord, she figured she could pull that apart too. It still wouldn't be easy, but trying to find straight sticks of the right height that were sturdy enough to support a tent through the night was never as simple as one would think. The forest was full of sticks, but each one was as unique and imperfect as a human.

"Sounds good to me." Jacks started moving around the rocks and Lucy bent over to help. They dug up what they could, moved anything loose, and brushed away as much debris as possible until they had a clear area to place the tent. There was one tree root, but Lucy knew they could avoid it if they placed the tent just right. While she'd never used a ZPacks Duplex, it was one of the most popular tents on the trail, so she was familiar with the ultralight, thin, blue design.

As Jacks started unloading his pack, she looked around and made a mental "to do" list. A nice patch of ferns caught her eye. They could gather those to place between the tent and ground for insulation. July or not, this far north the ground would still freeze them during the night. Next, they would need to unwind their paracord and pull the smaller string from the center. Paracord's beauty lay in its versatility. With seven small strings spiraled together and encased in a woven sheath, it possessed strength to hold a human, but removing the sheath revealed thinner strings that made excellent fishing line, thread, or tent guy-lines. With several hours before dark, they had enough time to settle everything before sunset without rushing.

JACKS

Jacks could tell that Lucy thought through things. He might not have known her for long, but she showed everything on her face. Already one of his favorite things about her, her transparency meant he didn't have to guess her motivation, intentions, or interest. He'd certainly noticed her eyes wandering across his chest earlier. The look on her face then had boosted his ego wonderfully.

Now, however, she studied the forest around them with an intensity that made him believe she solved all their problems right there in her head. He wouldn't rush her through that. She'd already proven she knew what she did out here. Once he'd unloaded most of his pack, he pulled off his emergency paracord bracelet. A whistle, a small cutting edge, and clip attached it around his wrist. He figured he might as well start unwinding it so they could use the paracord. The current length wouldn't hold up the tent, but he knew smaller strings hid inside it. That was the beauty of paracord.

Jacks easily found the end of the paracord, but breaking it loose from that first knot proved difficult. He tried poking at it in all kinds of ways. With longer fingernails, he could probably pop it loose. Thinking a stick might work, he found a small one and tried using it to shove the paracord end out of place. Instead, the stick snapped. Just as he grew frustrated and considered swearing and throwing the stupid thing at a tree, Lucy's laughter reached him. Looking up to see her eyes scrunched with delight at his dismay made everything better.

The frustration disappeared, and he found himself proud to have entertained her. He also decided this was a great time to suck it up and ask for her help.

At first, she happily took the woven band from him. They both realized the issue at the same time when she went to hold it with her left hand, so she could pull it apart with her right. The way her face fell crushed him just a bit, but instead of returning to frustration, he committed to making it work for her. So, he did.

Gently, he took back the bracelet but held it directly in front of her, so she could see where the end of the paracord was. "If I hold it, do you think you can pop it free from that knot?" he asked her.

"Maybe. It's harder when I'm not the one holding it."

"That makes sense. We could try another stick or maybe the end of my spoon?" Like most hikers, Jacks only carried one eating utensil. His titanium spoon was ten inches long and perfect for scooping out any kind of food that couldn't be eaten with his bare hands. He saw no need to cart around anything else but wasn't confident that it would be the right tool for this job.

The look on Lucy's face confirmed his thinking. "Wait, use my knife!" She pulled the knife from the sheath where it hung around her neck. He still hadn't gotten a chance to find out what happened that left her with nothing else, but he felt happy to see she had that. As he'd worked to lighten his pack over the years, he'd quit carrying one since he rarely used it. Another lesson learned, he supposed.

The tip of her knife provided exactly what he needed, and soon they both worked to pull out the inner strings. Jacks used the knife to cut open the outer covering while Lucy pulled the rest apart. She had sat down to lean against a tree again and would hold the cord between her knees while using her right hand to neatly separate the strings. The slow and tedious work required care to ensure it didn't all devolve into a tangled mess, but they made progress.

Partway through, Jacks realized they could wind the separated strings around small sticks to keep everything organized, so he helped with that as soon as he'd finished cutting through the covering. By the time they finished, they had seven sticks wrapped in decent balls of string. The string couldn't support the weight of a person, and even hanging a bear bag from it would pose a risk, but it offered the perfect weight for tying up the tent. He figured he could use two ties from each of the two peaks of the tent to hold it steady even if wind caught them during the night. He didn't expect major issues with the way they nestled into the hollow, but playing it safe beat taking risks. At that thought, his inner voice couldn't resist pointing out the irony of "playing it safe" while lost in the woods after crazy people had attacked him, while he carried no knife and had broken both his poles tumbling ass over teakettle down a hill.

Before he could spread out the tent, Lucy stopped him, "We should put ferns under the tent. They'll give us some cushion and insulation."

"Brilliant," he winked at her. "I'll go collect them."

Lucy huffed and smirked at him, "I'll get some too. I still have one good arm."

And the food had done a lot to improve her situation, Jacks noted with pride while nodding his agreement.

They tromped off in different directions to collect ferns, though he figured Lucy would carry significantly fewer since she had to pull and carry them all in one hand. When he turned back toward the tent, he spotted her with ferns protruding from every pocket. She had transformed herself into a beautiful ferny peacock with greenery fanning around her hips and knees. Fronds even decorated her ponytail, and when she bent to pick up a dropped cluster, more greenery burst from her back pockets. She carried even more than he did. The sight both amused and aroused him—wonderful but concerning since he'd share his tent with her. Thoughts of her snuggling next to him, her curves pressed against him, made him shift uncomfortably. His brain conjured the taste of her lips and the feel of her hair between his fingers. He quickly dropped his pile near the tent and turned to adjust himself discreetly.

When he turned back around, relief washed over him—she hadn't noticed anything. She already spread the ferns on the ground in overlapping layers. He left her to it and went for more ferns. They would combine their body heat in the tent, but without good insulation between them and the ground, they'd both freeze.

After collecting quite a pile, he helped her finish laying them out. Still not ideal, but as warm and comfortable as their circumstances allowed.

Setting up the tent just required working through it systematically. As Jacks tied the strings to tent and branches, he wished he'd spent more time learning different knots. His method wasn't pretty, and sometimes took a couple tries to get knots that wouldn't slip, but he managed.

He vowed to sign up for woodland survival courses after this ordeal—even if it felt like closing the gate after the cows had escaped.

Lucy had inflated his sleeping pad and piled things into the tent by the time he found a suitable branch and threw the line to hang their food. He wanted to let Lucy eat one more snack before tying it up. Rationing made sense, but she also needed energy to hike tomorrow.

"Hey, don't you need this?" Lucy teased him as she tried to hand him the food bag.

"Yeah, but you should pick out a protein bar or some jerky first." When she gave him a skeptical look, he tacked on, "We can share it."

She still frowned at him a bit, but she did pick out a Clif bar, unwrap it, and stare down at it while he put the wrapper in with his other trash. Out of the corner of his eye, he watched her contemplating how to break it in half to ensure he got his fair share.

"Just go ahead and eat what you want. I had breakfast this morning, remember? I'll have a bite in a minute." He didn't look at her as he hoisted the bag with the hope that she would follow her hunger if he didn't appear to be paying too close attention.

As soon as he released the stick that would catch on the bag and hold it twelve feet up and out away from any branches, she handed him about a third of the bar. That seemed to be as reasonable as he was going to get, so he took it and munched along back toward their tent.

"What kind of sleeping bag do you use?"

He hadn't even thought about it, but in this case, his ultralight supplies would work out okay for them. "I switched to a quilt about a year ago. I was able to get a wide version that was warmer than my old mummy bag but still a lot lighter. As long as you're okay with snuggling, we should be able to share it. It's not supposed to be too cold tonight anyway."

Backpacking quilts bore no resemblance to bed quilts. They resembled sleeping bags with the bottom half cut away from the knees up. Modern bag insulation provided zero warmth when compressed flat, making the extra material under a person's body wasteful in space, weight, and cost. The open design gave Jacks room to roll around in his sleep, stick out a leg when overheated, yet still strap down tight to his sleeping pad when needed. Even the wide version couldn't tuck around them both, but the night shouldn't get that cold. Simply draping it over them both like a loose blanket would keep them comfortable.

Lucy blushed. "I figured. I hope you don't mind snuggling." It was one of the rare times she looked vulnerable and possibly scared, or at least nervous about his reaction.

Jacks figured honesty was the best policy in this situation. "I don't mind at all. I'll ask before I touch and try my best to keep it respectful. I, uh," and this was where it got awkward. "I need you to know that I don't have any expectations, and I'm not going to 'try anything.'" He used air quotes and immediately felt like an idiot. At least he couldn't make it worse.

He continued, "I do find you attractive, and I, well my body, responds to that, but I don't want you to think that means that I expect anything or will do anything without your consent. I really respect how much you know about the outdoors, and I like your laugh, and I'm glad we're stuck out here together, so I'm not going to be a perv or anything." Aaaannd he was officially rambling like a lunatic.

Luckily, she seemed more amused than freaked out or offended.

Chapter 7

LUCY

After Jacks turned his spare shirt into her sling, neither of them had extra clothes. This wouldn't matter if she hadn't sweated during the day. As the sweat cooled on her clothing, it chilled her down too well. She started to shiver. She needed to get the shirt and sports bra off. Once she wiped the dried sweat off her body, she could probably put the shirt back on, but it would reek if she didn't hang it in a tree to air out overnight. That wouldn't end the world, but she didn't want to smell around Jacks. In fact, she favored smelling alluring while getting naked with Jacks.

The sun dipped toward the treetops, and Lucy felt ready to tell Jacks everything: what happened and what she'd seen. She hoped he'd have insight, but first she needed to stop shivering.

"I don't suppose you carry wipes or a cloth or anything. I need to go clean up enough to remove my dried sweat." Lucy was hesitant to ask him for anything, but he'd made it clear that he was happy to share with her.

"Oh yeah, I always carry a pack of wipes, but you're going to need help getting your shirt off." He studied her chest for a moment, but in a very clinical way. "I don't suppose your bra unhooks and comes off over your arms, does it?" He sounded like he already guessed the answer.

"No, I hadn't even thought about my wrist, but um, yeah, I'm definitely wearing a sports bra, though it's really stretchy," she added, hopeful that would help. She wavered about accepting help removing her shirt and bra. This certainly belonged to the category of experiences that had vanished from her life since losing Ben. The thought of another man's hands on her skin, even in this innocent context, meant crossing some invisible line she'd drawn around her heart. She chewed on the inside of her cheek as she considered letting Jacks help her out of her shirt and bra. She didn't hate the idea. In fact, part of her craved the simple human contact she'd denied herself for so long.

When she looked back up at him, she could tell that he sensed her nerves.

"How about we call you one of my clients. I'll help you the same way I would help them. No funny business," he held up three fingers, "scouts honor."

Lucy couldn't help but laugh at that, "That's the Girl scout sign! Boy scouts only hold up two fingers."

Jacks just shrugged and winked at her.

"Fine, okay." Lucy was tired of being cold, and Jacks had been nothing but completely respectful so far.

Jacks pulled out his wipes, set them on the ground beside them and moved behind her. He started by lifting the sling from around her neck and letting it hang from her elbow. As he started to lift the hem of her shirt, he talked her through what he was doing.

"Hold your left arm against your side to keep your shirt from pulling on it. We're going to stretch your shirt out and over your right arm first." His actions followed his words, and her good arm was soon free. "Now, we go up and over your head, so that we can pull it off your left arm with as little movement of your wrist as possible."

Jacks stayed behind her as they repeated the process with her bra. Lucy had never liked tight, constrictive bras, and she appreciated that this one had stretched enough to follow the same pattern they'd used with her shirt. While Lucy's wrist certainly hurt and the movement intensified the throbbing, Jacks's presence behind her never made her uncomfortable. She could almost sense the heat of his body, but he didn't lean into her, trail his fingers down her spine, or trace her tattoo with his tongue, even though she found herself vaguely wishing for all those things.

As soon as the air flowed directly across her skin, her shivering went from occasional to constant, and of course Jacks noticed.

He grabbed the wipes and handed one to her while offering, "Can I wipe down your back while you get your front?"

"Yes, p-please." Lucy's teeth were starting to chatter, but she knew how quickly she'd warm up once she was a bit cleaner.

"I love your tattoo." He read it aloud as he rubbed the wipe over it, "And one day she discovered she was fierce, & strong, & full of fire, & not even she could hold herself back." She could feel him taking extra time to clean the thorny rose that flowed through her Marc Jacobs quote, and let her head fall forward while she enjoyed the sensations of being cared for and admired.

"It's beautiful," he murmured, his voice softer now. "When did you get it?"

"After Ben died," she said quietly. "I needed something to remind me that I was still here. Still capable of being more than just half of something that was broken." She felt his hand pause against her back for just a moment, and she knew he understood what it meant to her.

"Well, it's perfect," he said, his voice warm with something that made her chest flutter. "It suits you perfectly."

"Looks like you're about done. Would you like to sleep in your shirt, your bra, or um, topless if that's how you'd be most comfortable?"

The way he tripped over the third option revealed his discomfort with it. Lucy suspected he was uncomfortable because he liked the idea, but it was too soon. This wasn't the right time or place. She had no interest in putting the sweaty, damp bra back on. "I suppose I'll be sleeping in my stinky shirt tonight."

"Okay, let me help get it back on and your arm back in the sling." He was close enough behind her now that she could feel the heat of his tall, broad chest. His chin was level with the crown of her head, making him the perfect height for her to lean back into. She knew he'd support her, too. If she were to lean back, she had no doubt his arms would come around and envelope her with his warmth, kindness, and care.

Lucy shook those thoughts away and worked with him to put her shirt back on and hang her bra up in a nearby tree to air out.

"Do you mind if I sleep in just my shorts?" he asked her.

"As long as you don't mind me sleeping in this shirt and my underwear."

"Works for me." This time there was just a hint of naughtiness behind his grin.

Lucy smiled, pulled off her pants, hung them with her bra, and stepped behind the tree to wipe down her remaining cracks and crevices. When she emerged, Jacks had wiped himself down and hung up his own shirt and pants. While Lucy had stayed barefoot since removing her hiking shoes and socks, Jacks had slid his bare feet back into his unlaced sneakers. Lucy glanced at his pack and realized he was missing a camp shoe, rendering its mate useless.

"Let me take the trash and wipes over and stick them in the bear bag. We probably should have done this part before hanging it for the night." Jacks blushed just a little, like he was embarrassed to have messed up his camp routine.

Lucy understood the feeling, but nothing had been routine that day. She pointed that out to him and climbed into the tent while he went off to finish stowing away the last of their smellables.

When he returned, they tried to share his sleeping pad. First, Jacks laid on it, and Lucy tried to lay beside him, but she kept rolling off and out from under the quilt. They switched it up, with Lucy laying on the sleeping pad, but that just led to Jacks rolling away. Eventually, they were both rolling with laughter as they joked about the sleeping pad's determination to keep them apart.

JACKS

Jacks ended up deflating the whole thing so that they could use it as a flat layer of insulation partially below each of them. He made sure that she was on his left so that she could lay on her right side and use his chest as her pillow without putting any pressure on her left arm. She hesitated for just a moment before resting her cheek against his heart.

Once she relaxed, and he could feel her warm breath ghosting across his skin while her long brown hair draped across her shoulder and down to tickle his bellybutton, he felt like this was what he'd been waiting for. He'd always focused on his career and trying to finish the AT without really taking the time to even look for love. Sure, he'd gone on dates and been casually involved with someone over the years, but it had never been important or felt meaningful to him. This felt different. It was like coming home to a place he'd never known existed. The way she fit against him, the trust she showed by letting herself be vulnerable, the quiet strength she carried even in her exhaustion. Everything about Lucy made him want to be better, stronger, more worthy of the gift of her presence beside him.

"Care to tell me about how you ended up here?" he asked her gently while using his right hand to play with the ends of her hair. He had already positioned her left wrist across his stomach and chest, supporting it comfortably for both of them. His left arm curved around her, holding her close.

Lucy sighed and tried to start a few times but couldn't seem to get her story going.

"When you left the shelter at lunch yesterday, you headed north, right?" he prompted.

"Yeah, and everything was normal. I stopped at Hell Hollow creek for water. I noticed it was unusually quiet but didn't think much of it." From there Lucy went on to tell him about the guns, Frank, and setting up camp with Grasshopper and Tag-a-long.

They quickly figured out that Grasshopper was the woman who came screeching out at Jacks, and Tag-a-long was the chickenshit who shoved him toward Frank. That didn't answer all their questions, but it did make it clear that those three were working together.

"None of that explains why, even what, they are doing out here though," Jacks commented thoughtfully as Lucy finished her story.

"Since whatever they're involved in requires hiding guns in the woods, I can see where they would want to get rid of me, especially if they know that I found the guns. But I don't understand why they left me alive in the woods and put my shoes on. I had assumed they left my knife because they didn't realize it was there, but I'm even questioning that now."

Lucy shifted from storytelling to analysis. Her breathing became more focused, more deliberate. He loved watching her mind work through the puzzle, the way she could compartmentalize fear and focus on logic even after everything she'd been through.

"Ok, let's think this through," he said, matching her analytical tone. "If you kill a person, you then have a body to deal with. A body on the Appalachian trail does not go unnoticed, and it would be obvious someone killed you." Lucy agreed with all of Jacks' points.

"But look at the story of Inchworm. Her body was just a little way off the trail, everyone was searching for her, and it still took two years before they found her body," Lucy pointed out. Everyone had been concerned when the sixty-six-year-old, experienced hiker had gone missing while stepping off the trail to relieve herself. No one expected it to take two years to find her body.

Jacks had been thinking of the exact same case, but he suspected they were drawing different conclusions from the comparison. As she brought it up, she'd sat up and was now playing with his chest hair while looking at him expectantly. They'd been huddled under the quilt long enough to overcome the chill of cleaning up and undressing, and their body heat was filling the tent. While the warm July air was cooling as the shadows lengthened, the temperature in the tent was very comfortable.

"Say they were familiar with Inchworm's story, how does that fit with what you're thinking happened?" he asked her.

"Well, all they had to do was dump my body in the same place they did anyway. Why not just go ahead and kill me? Why leave me alive and with shoes on?" Her head cocked to the side as she pondered her thoughts, and Jacks was struck by how beautiful she was. She'd unbraided her long, brown hair, so it hung down her shoulders in waves.

He also heard what she was saying. It was a good point, too. Leaving her body would have guaranteed that she couldn't tell anyone what she'd found. Jacks couldn't stand to imagine her body left lifeless, though.

"That makes sense. I was thinking that they'd followed the example more closely. By leaving you 'lost' with shoes on, I'm guessing they expected you to die 'naturally' of dehydration or starvation. That way, even if your body was found, it would just look like another lost hiker died in the woods instead of murder."

Lucy flopped back down beside him and then winced at the way it jostled her wrist. He'd used some sticks and more of his compression shirt to make a brace, but it was far from ideal.

"Easy, killer. I worked hard to limit the long-term damage to your wrist as much as possible. Don't go undoing all my hard work now." He gently lifted and inspected her arm while she settled her head back on his chest.

"Sorry." She sounded sad. "Your thinking makes the most sense, and all evidence points to them following that same train of thought. I just don't know what to do from here. I mean, I'm pretty confident I can get us out of the woods. Especially since we've got your supplies and water filter now, but then what? Obviously, we need to go to the police and alert the bubble of hikers making their way north, but I'm not even sure what to tell anyone beyond, 'There's a bunch of wackos that attacked me, and they are hiding guns in the woods.'" Lucy shook her head and huffed out her exasperation.

"You don't think that would be enough?" he asked incredulously as he rested her hand back on his sternum.

Lucy tilted her head back and rolled her eyes up to look at him. "You don't live in the country, do you?"

Jacks chuckled as he pointed out that most sports physical therapist work was found closer to a major city.

"That makes sense. What city do you live near?"

He thought back and realized that he hadn't ever mentioned it. "I'm just east of Pittsburgh. What about you? I know you're thru-hiking now, but what do you normally do for a profession?" It was becoming too dark to make out details, so he focused on combing his fingers through her hair.

Lucy hummed contentedly and relaxed even further into him before confessing, "I love having my hair played with. I know it's stupid, but it's one of my favorite things."

"Not stupid at all. Your hair is gorgeous."

"I'm trying to be a freelance graphic designer. Most of that work is online, and I can set my own hours. I was a school secretary to earn a regular paycheck. After Ben died, his life insurance gave me a nice nest egg. I rent out our old house, so I don't really have many expenses. In between adventures, I stay at my parent's place just outside Knoxville and do freelance work to earn a bit. I was feeling like I'd settle back down after finishing this trail. Now... I don't even know."

"I can understand that. My work expects me to show up again tomorrow. I'm not sure what they'll think when I don't. I've only been with this practice for about a year, and I'm not very close with anyone there. Eventually, I'd like to work for myself. It's a big leap, though."

Jacks' thoughts returned to the problems at hand, and he asked, "What did you mean when you commented that I must not live in the country?"

"Oh, just that guns being stored in the woods doesn't tend to warrant the level of panic city people like to imagine it does. A local sheriff might check it out if he or she is bored, but there are a lot of woods, and they generally have better things to do than go poking around behind and under random trees. The crazy people might get more of a reaction. But if they're well-known in the area, we might be blown off as overreacting outsiders." Lucy was wiggling around less, and her voice had gotten softer.

"We'll think about it more tomorrow." The tent was almost completely dark. It was time to sleep. Jacks couldn't resist kissing the top of her head. "Goodnight, Lucy," he whispered to her.

She sighed and whispered back, "I'm glad you're here. And not just for your stuff." There wasn't a single hint of teasing in her voice.

"Me, too."

Jacks remained awake and holding her for a while before he was able to doze off. He listened to the sounds of the night animals coming out to do their thing and thought about what they should do once they found civilization. As long as they were in the woods, he was confident that Lucy knew what they needed to do. Once they got into a town, he wanted to have a plan ready. First and foremost, they needed to find an emergency room or urgent care center that could x-ray, set, and cast her wrist. He was certain it was broken and was amazed that she was able to ignore it as much as she did. Then again, she'd survived the death of her husband, reclaimed her life, and taken care of herself through several adventures. That first day at lunch he'd noticed how strong and independent she was. It was hard to believe that was just yesterday. She felt like his best friend, well, best female friend who he was also very interested in. But he tried not to think too hard about that while wearing only his shorts with her pressed up against him. Eventually, he drifted off to the sound of her snuffles and thoughts of laughing and chasing her through the woods without a care in the world. He could picture them being blissful and relaxing and enjoying nature together.

Chapter 8

LUCY

L ucy's wrist hurt. Badly. Painfully. It was still dark out, but there was no way she could sleep any longer with the pain. No matter how she moved her arm, it never eased. The throbbing was just there, constantly battering at her ability to think and function. She closed her eyes and forced herself to relax her shoulders as she inhaled deeply through her nose before blowing it out through her mouth. More painkillers would be great, but they were hanging in the bear bag. She wasn't about to wake up Jacks to go get them. She didn't have shoes on and wasn't sure where he'd tucked his headlamp. Going to get them herself would just end with him awake, and her wrist possibly hurt worse. The moon was technically waxing now, but the sliver was so small, it was basically invisible.

So, she focused on breathing in and out. When Ben first died, she'd focus on her breath anytime she had been overwhelmed by everything that came with suddenly living a shared life all by herself. Even as she'd planned his service, she'd kept turning to ask his opinion or mention a detail she hoped he could take care of. It had been a hard habit to break, but she'd breathed through it and carried on one day at a time. She hadn't needed to tackle life like that in a while, but she was glad she had that experience now. In many ways, Ben had taught her what she needed to know to survive this whole situation. And then Jacks had joined her. Once again, she could turn to someone for help and support.

Lucy took another deep breath in and watched Jacks' chest hair wave in the breeze of her exhale. She closed her eyes on her next inhale and listened for the steady rhythm of his heart before breathing out again. It did nothing to lessen the pain in her wrist, but it fortified her soul to survive it. Once she'd found her equilibrium, she pushed her thoughts toward morning. Their food supply was limited. Most hikers carried three to five days of food with them, but that was if only one person was eating it. Jacks was already halfway through his planned hike, so Lucy figured he was down to just about one day of food left, maybe two if he carried extra.

She figured they could ration it and have something for each of them for the coming day and possibly one more. Her goal was to get them to a house or a road or something after no more than another two nights in the woods. That meant they needed to be on the move, and she didn't want to waste any of their energy.

She remembered being disappointed to hear that Jacks didn't bother to carry a paper map, though he did have a compass.

Most AT hikers ditched paper maps for GPS devices and apps like FarOut. Lucy almost did the same until she got lost in Arches without signal. Other hikers had rescued her then, but she vowed never to be dependent on that kind of help again.

She forced another breath and refocused. Jacks knew which side of the trail he'd landed on when he fled the privy. Since both shelter and privy sat on the west side, the trail lay east. They could bushwhack due east and hope to hit it, but then what? They'd still need to hike miles north or south to reach a road crossing. Worse, if they emerged between VT nine and Goddard Shelter, they'd be back in Frank's territory. This time, those men wouldn't bother making her death look accidental.

Following the water would be better. The wet leaves would become a trickle, then a stream. Water eventually led to people, and it would keep them from dehydrating. She closed her eyes, visualizing the map. National forest meant few roads or towns, but a second trail ran south from Goddard to some unpaved backroad. Three streams converged somewhere near there. If she remembered the topography right, following this water south would lead them to that convergence, that trail, that road, and eventually down to VT nine.

Shadows formed as the earth turned toward sun. The morning was still early but getting lighter. Bushwhacking would be brutal compared to maintained trail. They'd have to scout for the easiest path, fight through undergrowth, stop and repeat. At least following water gave them a clear direction, though streams could disappear underground without warning.

Jacks stirred beneath her, and she caught the shape of his body under their shared quilt in the growing light. The sight of him waking made her smile. Her grin widened when he kissed the top of her head and began to stretch.

"Hmmm, good morning." His voice was gruff with sleep still. "How's your wrist?"

She rubbed her face on his pec, gave it a chaste kiss, and wiggled her way up so her head rested more on his shoulder. "It hurts, but I'll be okay." She loved that his first thought of the morning was to check on her.

"What are your thoughts on getting us out of here today?" he asked as he started running his fingers up and down her arm while rubbing his chin on the top of her head.

"I don't think it's going to happen today, but I do have a plan. I was just thinking about the map, and I have a rough idea of where we might be and how to get us out. It will likely take us two or three days, though, depending on the terrain and how accurate my memory is. It could be a little longer than that." They didn't have enough food for longer than that. Even two or three days was stretching it thin.

"That works. Are we still following the water?"

"Yeah."

"So, no worries there. I think I have two hot meals left plus a couple packs of oatmeal and some snacks. Plus, I always carry extra trail mix. We can share an oatmeal for breakfast and one meal each evening and be good for two days. The third day and beyond, we might be living on the trail mix, but we should be okay for a while." Jacks didn't sound nearly as concerned about the food as she was.

"You really think it will be enough?" she couldn't help asking.

"Unless you have a secret stash somewhere, I think it is what it is. You've already proven to me that you know what you're doing navigating through here, so we'll make the best of what we've got. It'll be enough to keep us going." He was so matter of fact about it.

"We should probably get going then," she mentioned despite making no move to lift her head or roll off him.

He brought his right hand further around her so that she was fully wrapped in his arms. "I won't stop you from getting up if you want, but I vote we let the sun come up a bit more before we start staggering around camp."

"I am comfortable like this," except for her wrist, which she wasn't going to focus on.

"Good," he said in an oddly casual way before continuing, "I do really like you, you know. Not just in a 'we're both lost in the woods together' kind of way. I'm impressed by a lot about you." He kissed her head again.

"I like you, too." She looked up at him and tried to look kissable.

The goofy way he smiled at her made her think he might be laughing at her just a little.

But then he brought his lips to hers, and she decided he could laugh all he wanted if he kept kissing her. He wasn't forceful, and the kiss wasn't intense. It was a series of pecks and nibbles along her lips that woke up the butterflies living in her belly. She kissed him right back and ran her tongue along his bottom lip before nipping it with her teeth and making him moan. His hand moved up into her hair, so he could steady her head while he deepened the kiss.

JACKS

Lucy wasn't like anyone Jacks had ever met before. For one thing, her strength and resilience were astounding. If Frank and friends had any clue who they were really dealing with, there was no way they would have left her alive, but he was so grateful they did. He doubted he'd ever meet anyone like her again, and he sure as hell wasn't going to waste this opportunity.

He also wasn't going to rush it, though. He wanted her in his bed back in Pittsburgh, and he wanted her on the beach on vacation. He wanted her climbing on top of him with a fully healed wrist and snuggling in front of a fire in the middle of a snowstorm. So he pulled back, kissed her nose, looked into her eyes, and told her that she deserved an amazing dinner, a comfy bed, and his most gourmet breakfast in the morning.

"Until I can give you that and am confident I won't hurt your wrist, I will treasure every time you touch me, kiss you every time you let me, and make you smile as often as I can."

Lucy frowned, huffed, and tried to glare at him. Unfortunately for her, it just made her look that much more beautiful. He couldn't help grinning back at her.

"Fine," she agreed with resignation. "In that case, we should get up and moving, so that we can find that dinner and bed sooner rather than later."

"As you wish," he replied while helping her sit up.

From there, they both got busy with morning camp chores. Jacks loved how easily they'd been able to divide them up. They both dressed. Then Lucy had started picking up the inside of the tent while Jacks retrieved the food bag. He pulled out one of his two remaining packs of oatmeal along with two packets of instant coffee. It wasn't the best, but he always brought extra, so at least they had plenty of mediocre coffee. From there, he suggested that he pack up while she got breakfast going. He helped her back into the sling he'd made and checked that she had plenty of water before leaving her to it.

It didn't take him long to breakdown the tent and stuff everything back into his pack. She was just finishing mixing the coffee into the water remaining in the pot after mixing up the oatmeal when he sat down next to her.

She tilted the pot toward him, "Does this look okay?"

"Yeah, it's perfect."

She nodded at the smaller metal cup that doubled as a lid for his main pot. It was just the right size for one packet of oats. She handed him the spoon and asked him to stir it up.

"I never really feel hungry for breakfast, but I've learned it's tough hiking in the morning if I don't eat something," he commented as he finished mixing in the oatmeal and waited for it to thicken and cool.

"I'm the same way. I don't need much in the morning, but if I don't eat anything, I'm struggling by nine in the morning." Lucy sipped the coffee before offering it to him. He traded her the spoon and watched her balance the cup of oats on her knee while eating. *Good, she seemed steadier this morning.*

They finished breakfast quickly. Lucy rinsed and wiped dishes while he refilled their water bottles. They'd be following the stream, but he didn't want to risk thirst if the water became inaccessible. With limited food, staying hydrated mattered even more.

By the time dew began drying, they'd packed everything. He checked Lucy's makeshift splint and secured her sling, then turned his attention to her calf. She hadn't mentioned her shin yesterday, which either meant the stretching had helped or the wrist pain overshadowed everything else.

He convinced her to sit on his rain jacket on a fallen log while he settled onto his deflated sleep pad. Working her calf muscle, he found a few knots but nothing too concerning, despite her confession that she hadn't stretched the day before. Jacks glared at her over it, but her smirking response made his frown crack into a chuckle.

"In my defense, I was a little preoccupied with the whole lost in the woods thing."

"Fair enough," he answered, shaking his head. If he was counting on her to navigate them out, he'd happily take charge of things like filling their water, keeping their legs healthy, supporting her wrist, and feeding her as much food as he could convince her to eat.

Chapter 9

It amazed her how much easier today was than yesterday. Maybe she had slept better, not having been drugged; maybe it was not waking up and being surprised by her surroundings; maybe it was finding the water and having a clear direction; or maybe it wasn't any of those things. As she hiked along, she let the truth weave through her mind until she'd made peace with it. Jacks was the real difference. Yesterday, she had been scared, alone, angry, and ready to fight the world. Today she was powerful, cared for, and strong. It wasn't something she would have associated with joining forces with another person, but it was working for her, so she wasn't going to overthink it. It would be different with anyone else, but Jacks had strengths that seemed to fit perfectly with her weaknesses. Even better, he didn't try to overshadow her strengths, but instead rejoiced in them. He let her be her.

Lucy stopped to reorient herself and select their next destination. Breaking the hike down to simple tree to tree segments made up for the lack of a true trail. They'd been able to start the morning by walking almost directly on top of the wet leaves, but that had quickly turned into soggy mud that got piled up between bigger rocks. It hadn't been long before there was a full fledged trickle of water they were following.

"We should stop for a break and maybe a snack soon."

Lucy wasn't sure what to make of Jacks' request for a stop. Neither of them was out of breath, and Jacks had been encouraging her to drink water regularly. She couldn't imagine he really needed a break. "Are you okay? We haven't gone that far."

He sighed. "Yeah."

She waited and hoped he would explain more. Something was off. She started toward the next tree she was aiming for.

"I need to take care of you. I don't mean that you need me for that; I just don't like that you're doing all the work right now. I want to make sure you have a snack and maybe rub your leg, so it doesn't get knotted up. That's the part I know how to do. Plus, I've gotten a bit attached to you. I like knowing that I'm doing something to make sure you're okay."

And now Lucy couldn't be upset with him because he was trying to be nice. When they got to the next tree, she'd stop and let the two of them take a break. It might be a good time to start talking about what they would do once they made it out anyway.

It wasn't much farther. Lucy arrived at the point she'd been focusing on and turned to raise an eyebrow at Jacks. "Is this okay?" She might have thrown in just a touch of sass.

Jacks chuckled. "Yes, this is perfect. Do you mind stopping?"

Lucy didn't want to lie to Jacks, so she considered before answering him. "No, it's probably smart to take it easy. I'm just eager to cover ground."

"Makes sense. Here, take a couple Ibuprofen and drink some water. You shouldn't take it on an empty stomach, so why don't you have a small handful of trail mix."

She had to admit it was good to have him looking out for her. "You can rub my leg too, if you want." And she sounded like a stupid lovesick teenager now. "Never mind, that sounded worse aloud than I expected."

Her face scrunched up in embarrassment, but Jacks just laughed at her and teased, "So you want me to rub you now, huh?"

"Yeah, maybe I do." She wasn't sure this was the appropriate time or place to follow through with their teasing, but the flirting was good. "You've got great fingers. I bet you are good at rubbing lots of places."

"What can I say? I am a professional. Here, you eat, I'll rub." And with that, he handed her the baggie of trail mix and grabbed her calf.

As amazing as it was, Lucy was eager for them to cover ground. She believed in hoping for the best while preparing for the worst and was afraid that it might be closer to three days to the road. She wanted to do everything possible to get there sooner rather than later.

"I can see your worry, you know. You have an incredibly expressive face."

"Fine. I'm not confident about how far it is to the road, and we're moving incredibly slowly. It's making me nervous. I want us to either move faster or go farther or something."

Jacks kept rubbing her leg while he considered for a moment. "It's not safe for us to move faster. I've been watching the way you stop to pick our direction at regular intervals. It's smart, and it's kept us out of the worst of the undergrowth while letting us follow the water. We could hike for longer stretches, though."

"Good." Lucy puffed out her relief. "Let's get going." She handed him back the trail mix. She'd eaten a couple raisins and couple peanuts but not too much. She had taken the painkillers.

"I know you talked about looking for a particular spot where the water comes together. Any idea where that is in relation to the road?" He sounded more curious than hopeful.

"I don't know that I fully trust my memory of the map, but from what I remember, it's less than half the distance to the road. Though I'm not sure where we started from, so that could be off by a bit." Lucy considered for another second before confessing her worst fear, "Or I could be wrong altogether, and we could be somewhere completely different from what I'm thinking." Just thinking that made her hopeless. She didn't know what she'd do then.

"Hey." Jacks got her attention, and the look on his face showed her that her distress had been evident on her face. "It'll be okay. Tell me, if you had no idea where we were and had never seen a map of the area, what would you do?"

Immediately, she realized the point he was trying to make. "I'd go downhill to find water, and then follow the water to civilization." She'd told him that yesterday, and it was still true today.

"So, there's no reason to worry about where we are. The plan stays the same."

"I see your point. Thank you." She was better knowing that her potential failure didn't worry him. "I would like to try making it to the convergence of the streams tonight, though." That would reassure her that they were on the right path, plus it would give her a better sense of how long it would take them to reach the road.

"Alright. How about we walk until we reach that point or six in the evening, whichever comes first. Then we find a spot to make camp and dinner and call it a day."

"Seven in the evening before we stop, and it's a deal." Lucy wanted to make the most of each daylight hour they had.

"Six thirty." Jacks tried to counter, but Lucy just glared at him. "Fine, seven."

Lucy smiled and stood up. "Let's go."

As much as her wrist hurt, walking without a pack had her light and free. She tried to enjoy the increased agility but still had to be mindful that she only had one good hand to catch herself or grab onto things with. So, she plowed forward with careful steps.

Jacks continued to insist that they stop often for water, and Lucy was fine with that. She did refuse to sit down, though. Finding a seat and getting up and down off the ground was a waste of time and effort she wasn't willing to accept. The water was now a stream that bubbled over rocks and cut corners into the ground as it wound its way down the mountain. She knew they were making progress and believed they should be spotting the other two streams anytime now.

That thought kept circling on repeat through her brain, anytime now, anytime now, anytime now. It adopted the same rhythm as her footsteps, and she was struggling to focus on moving from one tree to her next destination tree. She was distracted by searching her surroundings for signs of more water.

JACKS

He could sense Lucy's rising panic. Her methodical steps adopted an air of frenzy, and her laser focus had shifted to distraction. Eventually, he realized that she was struggling to even stay focused on the tree that she was aiming for. He watched as her straight lines became meandering, even though she was stepping faster and faster. The big question was what to do about it. Was she distracted by pain in her wrist? Did she need to eat more? At one point, she stopped suddenly, held up her hand for quiet and listened hard before looking all around.

That was when he realized the truth. She was doubting herself and the course she had set for them. There was no doubt that limited food and excessive pain were making it worse, but the root problem was her anxiety over their location and direction of travel. But again, what could he do to help?

When he heard how fast her breathing had become, he decided that any course of action would be better than letting this continue, so he stopped them.

"Hold up a minute, Lucy," he called calmly over her shoulder.

"Do you seen one of the other streams?" she immediately asked as she turned around.

Now he had confirmation. "No, but that doesn't matter. We are headed south. We will hit Route Nine. It doesn't matter when or what we see along the way. I can sense your anxiety. Let's just stop for a minute and chill."

"No, we should keep going."

"Lucy. Stop." He sighed. He just wanted to hug her and reassure her that it would all be okay. Maybe that was even what she needed. "Come here."

Lucy gave him a confused look.

"Can I just..." he was stupid asking for a hug while lost in the woods. "Will you just come here, please?"

As Lucy stepped closer, he opened his arms, and she walked right into them.

"It's okay," he reassured her. "We've got this. Together, we will be okay." He heard the first of her sniffles and kissed the top of her head.

"What if it isn't? What if I'm wrong, and we end up stuck out here forever?"

"You aren't wrong. I know you're not. You've found water for us, and you figured out which side of the trail we're most likely on. It's going to be okay." He needed her to stop crying. It reminded him of the way his grandmother had cried when he first arrived at her bedside before she'd died. She'd tried to apologize for interrupting his hike.

He hugged his arms tighter around Lucy and her breathing became slower and deeper. She was angled to keep her bad wrist from being squished but wrapped her good arm around his waist between his back and his pack.

As she settled down, she asked, "Why aren't there any flowers here?" which just confused Jacks even more.

"What do you mean?" Maybe she'd snapped and gone bonkers. He'd heard of such things happening to hikers lost in the woods.

"There were tall purple flowers scattered all around on the east side of the trail. I saw them when I went to dig a cathole but never got a chance to check them out up close. There's nothing like that over here. Something was off to me for a while, but it was just as I was standing here with you that I realized exactly what the issue was. Why aren't we seeing any of the purple flowers?"

He considered the picture he'd taken instead of clipping a flower for her and saw her point. Then again, mountains were funny features that often presented very different faces. "Maybe they only grow on the eastern side of the mountain. You said yourself that we're likely on the western side."

Lucy stepped back out of his arms with a seriously thoughtful look as she wiped the tears from her face. "But wouldn't we see them on the eastern side of that mountain?" She pointed at the ridge rising in front of them.

She had a point. They were walking through a hollow between the eastern side of one mountain and the western side of another. It would make sense for them to see the flowers growing on the eastern side of this mountain. Jacks looked around but the purple flowers they'd seen before had been obvious. There were none in this area.

"Any idea what kind of flower they were?" Jacks didn't have a clue about identifying anything beyond poison ivy but was hopeful Lucy had better prepared herself with plant identification the same way she'd been smart about developing her navigation skills, survival skills, and taken the time to get familiar with a map of the area.

"No. They aren't anything I'm familiar with. And I think it's odd that they seem to only grow in that one specific area. I wish I'd grabbed one to study more closely."

Jacks smiled as he considered his vision of presenting Lucy with one of the beautiful blossoms. "I wanted to give you one but settled for just taking a picture of it. It was on my phone though." He was disappointed to realize the picture was gone. It might be useful to have.

"You don't back it up to the cloud?"

"Well, yeah, but I don't have access to it right now. Plus, I'm not sure if I had enough service for it to sync after I took the picture."

Lucy sighed. "Fair enough. Sorry about my freak out. This whole situation just seems off to me."

"You mean beyond finding guns, getting drugged and dragged off into the woods to die, and getting attacked?"

Lucy rolled her eyes at him and huffed. "Let's just go, so that we can get to the road and report all this crap." She started leading the way off through the trees again.

"About that." Jacks had been considering that they might need to be careful about how they reported everything and who they talked to. "Who do you think we should report it to?"

"I hadn't really considered it. I just figured we'd talk to a sheriff or state trooper or somebody. It might even be that we report it to a forest ranger assuming we're still in the national forest."

Jacks left it at that. It was midafternoon and hot. He tried not to overthink anything, but there was a lot bothering him. As he walked, he considered everything they had both been through. The flowers were important. He knew they had to be. He just wasn't sure how or why. As a child, his grandmother had forbidden him from crossing onto the land of one particular neighbor. Once he'd hit his teenage years, that had been more like a dare than a warning, so of course, he'd gone exploring. When he'd found himself surrounded by neat rows of identical plants, he'd quickly learned to identify marijuana. These plants had been nothing like that. There was a clear stalk with vibrant green leaves and single purple flowers with wide petals.

Lucy had been right about them being obvious. That meant they were either innocuous or local authorities were involved in whatever was happening. He paused for a moment to watch Lucy find the next tree to focus on. She appeared calm and steady, so he went back to his considerations while following along behind her.

He decided to start with what he knew. Lots of people do lots of illegal things in the woods. Growing weed was out. He knew what that looked like. Illegal liquor stills were still an option. The guns could be there to protect the moonshine business, and they just hadn't seen any of the stills for themselves. That would leave the flowers out, not impossible, and would explain three people roaming around, loosely connected, but all watching out for each other.

Their reaction hadn't been to simply kill them, though. They'd turned Lucy into a "lost hiker." The natural response to that would be people combing through the woods looking for her. While stills could be well hidden, if even one person stumbled on one, it would be obvious it didn't belong, and that person would report it. Unless a lot of locals were involved. Jacks frowned. That was unlikely at best. His considerations were wandering away from logical and into crazy town.

He looked up toward the horizon and found the sun sitting off to their right. It reassured him that they were headed south. There was no doubt about that. It was also moving from afternoon into evening. They'd keep walking for another couple hours, but it wouldn't be too much longer before it was time to stop. This was probably a good time for another quick water and rest break before they pushed through to wherever they were going to make camp for the night. The ground wasn't as steep as it had been earlier in the day, but it was rocky. They would need to take time to find a spot for their tent.

Chapter 10

LUCY

She was working hard to keep her footsteps steady and not get worked up. Several times, she heard a trickle or burble of water from the side of them opposite the water they were following. Secretly, she was hopeful they were about to find the convergence, but she wasn't letting herself get worked up about it. Jacks had been right to point out the futility of that. Finding or not finding the spot that she might remember wouldn't change anything. So, she kept walking.

The sound was becoming more and more noticeable, though. She finally broke down and stopped for a moment to look around.

"Oh, good. I was just about to suggest we take a water break," Jacks chimed in oblivious to what she was noticing.

"Hold on. Listen for a minute. Do you hear anything?" She turned around to watch his face.

He took her request seriously, and she could see the moment that he heard it also. "Is that water?"

"I think so. Can you stay here for a second while I go look around?"

"Stay within sight of me so we don't both end up lost separately, please."

Lucy couldn't help but chuckle. She suspected Jacks was more concerned about himself getting more lost, but she knew his concern was valid. "Don't worry, I don't plan to go far."

She wandered a few yards toward the noise before seeing what she was looking for. There was a drop off that she couldn't see over, but she could hear water beyond it. Rather than continuing on for a closer look, she turned back toward Jacks. They would find it for themselves soon enough. This had been enough to ease her worries and assure her that she was exactly where she had calculated she was.

"Yeah, I think we're almost to the convergence of the streams. Let's keep going."

"Have a drink first, and then we'll keep going."

She smiled at him. With her nerves settled, she was able to fully appreciate his care for her.

It only took three more trees before they spotted the waters coming together. There were two tiny streams, including the one they'd been following, that joined to form a creek that rushed and flowed and was wide and deep enough to require rock hopping to cross. Lucy was ecstatic. If she was right about this and remembered the distances correctly, they'd need to hike all day tomorrow but should hit the road around lunchtime of the following day. They would run out of food, but not long before they found the road.

They needed to cross one of the tiny streams to continue following the larger creek. Lucy was worried about keeping her balance with one bad wrist. If she slipped on a rock or leapt and landed wrong, she'd only have one hand to catch herself with. The stream wasn't wide or deep, but the mud on both sides was the kind of mud that Vermont was famous for. It would suck down her shoes and refuse to let go, and that was if she managed to avoid slipping and falling.

Jacks stepped in front of her and hopped neatly across without the slightest stumble. Just as she was about to attempt the same, he dropped the pack and turned around.

"Hold on," he said while lifting one foot to remove his shoe and sock. Then he stuck that naked foot right down into the muck as an anchor point and offered her his arm. With that added stability, she leapt across without hesitation. It took him a minute to clean off his foot enough to redress it, but she didn't mind waiting. It was a beautiful spot. If not for the mud and excess of thorny bushes, she might consider suggesting they stop here for the night.

As it was, she was glad they had a couple hours yet to find a better place to set up the tent. She found the next tree she would aim for while he situated the pack, and off they went. Lucy knew that nothing had really changed, and yet, her confidence returned as her doubts receded. Several of the patches of thorns turned out to be berry bushes, so she and Jacks snacked on some as they moved along.

She was weaving them between the trees avoiding sticker bushes when she heard a branch to her left suddenly snap. It was too loud and isolated a sound to be a scurrying squirrel or a stealthy deer. Snaps like that were usually caused by black bears, and that is exactly what Lucy saw when she looked over. This was not her first, or even her third, time looking up and into the snout of a black bear.

Usually they bolted as soon as they spotted her. The one exception had been a bear so focused on ripe blackberries that it barely acknowledged her polite request to keep eating berries instead of her while she walked briskly away.

In general, black bears didn't care about humans. They were more interested in food than anything else, so unless there was food involved, bears and hikers were able to happily coexist.

There was only one exception to this concept of happy coexistence. The term "mama bear" had not come about by accident. The first thing any smart hiker did when spotting a bear was check around to find any nearby cubs to ensure that they did not end up between the cubs and the bear. That was about the only way to guarantee a scuffle with a black bear.

"Look for cubs," she whispered to Jacks, keeping her eyes on the big bear. Then she added, "Quietly."

Soon he whispered back, though his words were laced with panic. "Shit! Um, Lucy, there are two cubs to our right. We are about to walk directly between them and Mom."

"Yeah, kinda figured that would be our luck."

"I'm going to grab the back of your shirt to guide you, and we're going to back away slowly together. If Mom looks like she's going to charge, I'll step up beside you so we can look as big as possible."

"Kay." Lucy wasn't exactly holding her breath, but she certainly wasn't inhaling and exhaling easily.

She felt Jacks' tug on her shirt and started to step back. Her left foot hit toe first, and she rolled back onto it as she picked up her right foot. Carefully and slowly, she followed Jacks' gentle pull backward until they were far enough away that she could see both Mom and cubs at the same time. The mama bear dropped to all fours and huffed at them while stomping her foot. She still wasn't pleased.

Lucy felt Jacks pulling her back further, but before she could take another step the mama bear's snout dropped just a fraction, and she began to charge directly toward Lucy and Jacks.

JACKS

Oh, hell, no! Jacks was not about to let that bear anywhere near Lucy. By the time he'd finished his thought, he'd already grabbed her around the waist and scooped her around one hundred eighty degrees, so that she was tucked into his chest while he had his back to the bear. Part of him knew that he should push her away so that she could run while he fought. But he was too instinctively selfish. He wanted her to stay with him.

When he was able to breathe in freely and didn't feel claws at his back, he knew it had been a bluff charge. Maybe that was why he hadn't made Lucy run; it certainly sounded better than saying he was selfish and wanted to feel her wrapped in his arms.

Though now that she was in his arms, he'd be happy to keep her there.

Another huff from the bear reminded him of the bigger picture, and he forced his brain to change course.

"What now?" he whispered in her ear, hopeful that she could see around him to determine what the bear was doing.

"Um," she wiggled her face under his arm, and he could hear the pain in her voice. Shit, he was an asshole. He hadn't even considered her wrist. He loosened his grip on her.

"Okay, I can see her now." Lucy's was as soft of a whisper as his had been. "She won't take her eyes off us, and she's pacing a bit. We need to back up more." Lucy started to pull away from him.

"Hold on. I'm going to pick you up and move us farther away while you keep an eye out over my shoulder." He didn't give her a chance to respond before he turned her so that her good arm was against him and scooped one arm under her knees. Like most long distance hikers, she was lean and light. As a section hiker, he didn't spend enough time on the trail to drop much weight, but he did have a regular appointment at the gym to keep in trail worthy condition. He'd learned the hard way that the first day of hiking would kick his ass if he didn't keep up a hefty workout routine.

He felt Lucy's chin poke into his collarbone as she peered over his shoulder and reported in, "She stopped pacing and is looking back and forth between us and the cubs." Jacks kept walking. "Now, she's heading over to her babies. She's not even looking at us anymore."

He was relieved to be out of danger, but they'd still need to find a way through the area. It's not like they could just decide to hike in a different direction. They also needed to put distance between themselves and the bears before they made camp for the night.

"You can put me down now," Lucy interrupted his thoughts.

He looked ahead and spotted a large boulder with a mostly flat top that only had a little moss on it. He carried her over there and sat himself down with her in his lap. She started to wiggle, but he tightened his hold.

"Can we just sit like this for a minute?" he asked her.

Lucy's face became very serious as she looked directly at him. "Are you okay?" she finally asked.

"Yeah." He took a moment to consider what exactly was going on with him. "I don't want to let go of you right now. That bear..." he was struggling to figure it out and explain it to her.

"We're ok," she tried to reassure him.

"I know. Its... I..." he huffed in frustration and decided to start babbling and hope she could make sense of it. "I was four when my dad said goodbye and never came back. My mom started using drugs. When I was in kindergarten, I told everyone she was sick. I thought it was like cancer, and I guess it kind of was. Early into first grade, a guy showed up at our house and ripped the place apart. He hit her and threatened us. That was when my grandmother stepped in and had me come live with her. My mom overdosed about a year later. School was rough, and I wasn't the greatest kid, but Gram kept me moving forward. I didn't manage to make friends until I got to college, though. That's when I met Collin, that hiking buddy I've told you about. Anyway, when that bear started to charge, I imagined losing you. I know we just met, and we don't even really know each other that well, but..." Jacks shrugged and rubbed his cheek on her head. "I need you to be okay. The bear scared me, and I didn't like it."

Lucy leaned her head more fully against his chest and sat quietly. Eventually, she whispered to him, "I can hear your heartbeat. It's finally slowing down to a calm rhythm."

He realized she was right. Earlier, his heart had been pounding a furious beat, but now it was settled. He smiled, "Yeah. Thanks. So, what should we do now?"

"We need to be farther from the bears before we make camp. I'm betting they enjoy these berry bushes as much as we did." She pulled away from him enough to nod at the bushes they'd snacked on as they'd passed through earlier.

"Any idea on how to get through there?" He'd bushwhacked around bears before, but never a mama with two cubs who was already agitated.

"We should cross the creek. It'll give us some space while still moving in the right direction."

"Don't black bears love water?" he asked her skeptically. This seemed like one of those plans that wasn't really a plan but might act like a placebo to make you think it was safer than just walking right up to the bear.

Lucy shook her head and chuckled before pointing out, "Yes, bears do love water, but there aren't many berries over there, and even if we do have to pass them, we're less likely to end up between her and her cubs."

Lucy's logic won again, and he bowed to her brilliance. Well, he tried to bow to her but somehow when he looked into her eyes, smiled, and dipped his head, he ended up pressing his lips to hers. From there, they worked together until she was straddling him, so that both of them could easily taste each other's lips. Jacks loved tasting the sweet tang of their earlier berry snack when she let his tongue slip inside and tangle with hers.

She had a strong grip on the nape of his neck, and he kept one arm tucked tightly under her ass so she wouldn't slip while the other wrapped around her sleek back. He shifted his lips from her mouth to her jaw, leaving little nips as he worked his way down to her neck. She smelled like summer and tasted like sunshine. It was obvious that she didn't wear sunscreen, lotion, or makeup. When he allowed his tongue to reach out and touch her skin, he could taste hints of the forest mixed with the light, salty flavor that came with warm weather hiking.

Lucy's moan was a deep rumble that he felt through her throat as she kneeled up and curled her head over his. He wanted so badly to explore all of her, to reassure himself that she really was okay, and here with him, and real. As much as he wanted to wake up and discover that being lost in the woods was just a bad dream, the thought of Lucy disappearing as well made the thought of waking up feel like a nightmare. He loosened his hold on her and reduced his kisses to soft pecks while he rested his head on her shoulder and took a few deep breaths. Her cheek was resting on top of his head as she hugged his neck.

Eventually, she lowered one foot to the ground and then the other. Jacks kept his hands on her waist as she stood, and he followed. He still had the pack fully strapped to his back, but he kept his balance and lifted one hand to cup the side of Lucy's face.

"I think meeting you has turned being lost in the woods into my favorite adventure," he confessed while tucking a stray strand of hair behind her ear.

Lucy's eyes shifted back and forth, and Jacks stepped back to give her space. Maybe it wasn't the same for her. Maybe he was just there; maybe she needed his supplies.

"Logan," Lucy's use of his real name startled him enough to refocus on her, "You are important to me, too. I just always thought Ben was it for me. I can't imagine finding someone else."

"It's okay, Lucy. I understand."

"No, you don't. I'm saying that I really like you. Like, I really like you, and it feels good with you. I feel good with you. This whole mess. It's okay. Because you're here, too."

"I feel like there's a 'but' coming." He would be nice no matter what. She deserved that.

"I don't know if there's a 'but' or not. That's part of what I'm trying to say. I could throw caution to the wind and fall head over heels in love with you right this minute, but I don't know that it would last. And I think that whatever I have with you, I want it to last for a long time."

Lucy was looking down at her feet now, so he tucked his pointer knuckle under her chin and gently tilted her face back up to his.

"Are you asking me to take it slow?" he teased her with an underlying air of seriousness.

She gave him the grin he was hoping for before replying, "Yeah, I think I am."

"Then I guess we should make sure both of us survive this adventure, shouldn't we?" He took her hand in his and led her over to the creek to find a place to cross. "Just like before, I'll take the pack across and come help you. Wait for me."

"You're worth waiting for," she replied as he realized what he'd said.

"So are you," he added as he released her hand and stepped from one rock to another until he could lean the pack against the base of a tree, remove his shoes and socks and wade back into the water to give her a hand.

Chapter 11

LUCY

Once across the creek, they were able to continue their descent beside the water. This side was full of much thicker underbrush. Lucy held a stick in front of her face to knock down the bazillion spiderwebs woven between saplings as she did her best to lead them onward. It turned into less of a tree-to-tree adventure and more a game of 'where can I put my foot next?' The shade was thick, which was nice, but it also meant darkness would descend more quickly. There was no hope of finding a place to put a tent here. Lucy constantly found herself leaning against trees to take a break from the steep sideways slant of the land. The few times that she lost her footing and started to slide Jacks always caught her. He'd make sure she was steady and stable before removing the warmth of his hands from her ribs or waist.

Their pace slowed enough to make a snail feel fast, but they eventually made it beyond where they'd encountered the bears. Unfortunately, now there was nowhere to easily recross the water, so they continued forward. When Lucy started to hear the songs of night insects coming out to play, she called over her shoulder, "Any ideas on where to camp?" Maybe he'd seen something she'd missed.

"Not through here. We need to keep going. I have a flashlight and a headlamp if we need them. Both should have full battery power."

At least there was that. Lucy didn't mind hiking at night, but she preferred a full moon over the tiny sliver they hoped to see tonight. She also struggled to imagine how difficult it would be to traverse this terrain by the light of a headlamp. She'd been known to trip over rocks and roots when night hiking on a well maintained trail. This would be much worse.

Even those challenges and worries weren't enough to drown out the rumble of her stomach, though. While she'd been hungry most of the day, her abdomen was beginning to feel so empty it was making her queasy. She wasn't shaking, but she could tell that she didn't have the same level of coordination that she did before.

"Lucy, can you keep going for a bit longer? It looks like it might open up ahead. We might be able to find a spot there and at least make some food." Jacks' question made her realize that she'd almost completely stopped her forward progress.

"Yeah, I'm okay," she focused on putting one foot in front of the other.

Jacks had a good eye and had been correct. There was a powerline, and the power company had cut a clearing through the forest to run the lines. The buzz from the lines wasn't the ideal white noise for sleeping, but it gave them a decent place to eat and camp. Lucy started to plop down on a rock, but Jacks grabbed her.

"Hold up. We need to check for snakes."

She knew that. A rocky outcropping in a clearing like this was their ideal place to sun themselves, but she just wanted to sit down. The day had done her in. Between the stress of navigation, limited food, a bear encounter, and a small emotional breakdown, she needed to eat and sleep.

A quick check around and under the rocks showed that they were clear of reptiles. There was enough clearcut space to put up their tent but nowhere to tie up the top peaks.

"We can use the power pole for anchors," Jacks suggested.

Lucy grimaced. It wasn't a smart choice, and she worried about how exposed they were. She hadn't seen a weather report in several days and wasn't confident enough with the area to make predictions based on the sky alone. She didn't think it would storm, but there were a few clouds in the sky, and July was not known for calm and peaceful evening weather. As long as there was no lightning, they should be fine. If a storm blew over, though, they'd need to get away from the big metal tower in the open clearing.

With the strings still attached from the night before, setup went quickly. Jacks fired up his stove on a flat rock while

Lucy watched for the boil. They'd moved away from the creek following the powerline, but finding water in the morning meant simply walking downhill.

Lucy kept an eye on the stove, poured the appropriate amount of water into the dehydrated meal pouch when it was ready, and let Jacks handle setting up the bedding inside the tent. There was a bit of wind blowing through the clearing. It wasn't enough to be bothersome, but it did cool things down quickly as the sun dipped behind the horizon. By the time dinner was soaking to rehydrate, she was starting to shiver.

That was the same time that Jacks popped out of the tent with his food bag and bear line along with wipes. With no clean clothes to change into, they would want to climb straight into the tent and under the quilt once they'd cleaned up. Being out in the open also meant that they didn't have a bed of ferns to insulate under their tent. The sun should have warmed the ground enough for it to be okay, but Lucy wasn't expecting it to be her best night's sleep.

"I'm going to throw the line for the bear bag. This way, as soon as we eat, we can clean up and climb into the tent," Jacks told her as he set down the food bag and headed for the tree line with his rock sack and rope. He'd put a few small rocks in the sack tied to the end of the line to make it easier to aim over a branch. Once the line was hung over the branch, he could go back to it later and just clip on the bag and hoist it into the air. By throwing the line now, he was getting the hard part out of the way.

"Food should be ready in another five minutes," Lucy had just stirred the bag. It looked like it was rehydrating well, and the chicken and pasta smelled amazing. Dehydrated chicken wasn't one of her favorites, but the pasta always turned out great, and she was hungry enough to happily ignore any spongy chicken bits. Hopefully, the hot food would help warm her up, too.

Jacks had filled the pot with more than enough water for the meal. Warm liquid running down her throat and filling her belly to heat her from the inside out sounded blissful. She looked around for a moment before sniffing a few times. What sounded best was a nice cup of hot tea, and she knew how to make that happen even in situations like this. After sniffing a few more times, she admitted to herself there was no mint in the area. It was one of the plants she'd never find with her eyes, but her nose could identify it from one hundred yards away. This was the wrong part of the country for sage. There was no reason to waste any energy looking for it, but she did spot some dandelions in the area. They made for bitter tea she didn't particularly care for, but it would be something. She just couldn't decide if she'd rather have bitter tea or plain hot water.

She was reminding herself of the many reasons she never drank coffee before bed when Jacks returned and opened the food bag with a giant grin on his face.

"What are you smiling about?" she asked suspiciously.

"I was just thinking it might be nice to share a cup of hot cocoa with our meal this evening." He winked at her as he pulled out two packets of Swiss Miss.

He held them both up and continued, "I have two, but I'm thinking it might be better to share one tonight and save the other." Then he waited to hear her thoughts.

As much as she'd love to have an entire packet to herself, he was right to ration it. "That's probably the best idea. We covered a good distance today, but I think we'll probably have one more night out here before we hit the road. We can add extra water. I don't mind weak cocoa." Any sweet flavor would be a big step up from the hot water, bitter tea, or sleep preventing caffeine she'd been contemplating a few minutes earlier.

"Weak hot cocoa coming right up. You check the food, while I mix it up." Jacks tucked the second cocoa packet away and stirred the first into hot water. He passed her the spoon, and she ate the creamy chicken pesto pasta slowly, letting each bite settle. The hot chocolate warmed her hands when she traded him the spoon.

Food and warmth spread through her chest. Stars began appearing one by one as sunset colors faded. She leaned against Jacks, bumping his shoulder with hers. Despite everything that had gone wrong, this felt right. Just the two of them, basic survival, and the night sky opening above them.

JACKS

Jacks settled beside Lucy, savoring the quiet meal under the emerging stars. The wind picked up, and he shivered.

"You must be freezing," he said, noticing how still she'd been sitting. "Here, finish this." He handed over his remaining pasta.

"Thanks." She passed him the cocoa in return. "This'll warm you up."

As soon as they finished eating, Jacks rinsed the pot and packed everything except the wipes.

"Ready for the wipe-down dance?" Lucy asked, less hesitant than the night before.

He enjoyed the sensation of her skin under his hands as he helped her remove her shirt and bra. Then he briskly rubbed warmth up and down her arms while she finished cleaning up and stripping down to her shirt and underwear.

"Go hop under the quilt in the tent, and I'll be right there," he told her as he started to strip off his own hiking clothes. It was fully dark now and the sliver of moon was hiding behind a few clouds.

Jacks pulled on his headlamp and made quick work of hanging clothes and securing the food bag to the rope.

A coyote howled in the distance as he hoisted the bag into the air. The sound didn't unnerve him tonight. It was too far away to threaten him but gave life to the forest that would have otherwise felt empty and lifeless.

He slipped into the tent and zipped the vestibule. The electrical tower's buzzing would be white noise tonight, nothing more.

"That tower was perfect for hanging clothes," he murmured as Lucy snuggled against his chest.

"The wind should freshen things up, too," Lucy murmured, already half asleep.

"Goodnight, Lucy," he whispered before kissing the top of her head and allowing his own eyes to fall shut.

Jacks wasn't sure what time it was, but he was not excited to wake up to someone frantically shaking him awake. There was no way it could be morning already. Then he heard Lucy's voice, "Jacks! Logan, get up! We need to move! Get up, Logan! We have to go, now!"

Her frantic insistence had him shaking off his mental cobwebs and bolting upright. "What's going on?" Were Frank and his buddies coming after them? Was there a bear? While Lucy had certainly gotten him to wake up and pay attention, Jacks still wasn't sure what he was supposed to be paying attention to.

"There's lightning. We need to get out from under this tower."

Jacks took just a second to listen for rain. When he didn't hear any, he ignored the flash of light and listened for thunder. Lucy was starting to unzip the tent, but he stopped her.

"Wait just a minute. Have you heard any thunder?"

She furrowed her brow and considered while Jacks continued to listen. After a second, she shook her head "no."

"Good, that means the lightning is too far away to be dangerous, yet. We should move the whole tent into the tree line now before the storm blows this way. Climb out, and I'll wrap the quilt around your shoulders, so that you can carry it and the sleeping pad. Then I'll move the tent." Jacks didn't want her trying to juggle too much in her arms.

Lucy nodded her understanding, crawled out of the tent, and stepped into her shoes. Jacks followed her and draped their bedding over her shoulders before strapping the headlamp to her forehead.

"Do you have your flashlight?" she asked him.

"No. I'll be fine to follow you as long as you don't go too far ahead of me."

Lucy waited patiently and aimed the headlamp at the knots while Jacks untied the tent from the tower and pulled up the stakes. He wadded the whole thing up and they headed for the trees. There really wasn't anywhere good to set up, and he didn't want to risk ripping his tent. They looked around for a bit before Lucy spotted an area that wasn't too bad. The trees were too close together for him to stake the tent tightly and tying the top of it up would be tricky. But Jacks could make it work. It wouldn't be perfect, but it would give them shelter to stay dry.

They heard the first rumbles of thunder just as Jacks tied up the second string. He hadn't staked anything down yet, but that only took another moment. The tent was saggy, so they wouldn't be able to stretch out or move around inside. Hopefully, the wind wouldn't get any worse. Jacks helped Lucy into the tent before asking for the headlamp and making a mad dash back to grab their pack. There wasn't much of anything in there, but if the pack got wet, it would be heavy and would soak anything and everything they tried to pack into it in the morning.

Once he had the pack tucked under the one wing of the vestibule that he'd managed to stake out, he huddled inside. The only way he and Lucy both fit without the tent draping over them was to spoon on their sides with their knees pulled up. As much as he loved laying behind her, his arm quickly went numb from the weight of her head and his legs started to cramp up. Based on the small wiggles he was experiencing, he could tell that Lucy was similarly uncomfortable. But neither of them complained. They were dry, as safe from lightning as they could be, and the storm seemed to be moving quickly.

The wind did whip up, and the rain came down in sheets. For about a quarter of an hour or so, the two of them clung to each other in tense silence. Jacks was terrified the tent wouldn't hold up. It was designed to be staked out tight. The loose balloon they were currently huddled inside was being yanked and pulled by the storm. Thankfully, the system passed quickly, though neither he nor Lucy were managing to fall back to sleep.

"I was worried the tent wouldn't hold up through the wind," he confessed to her in the predawn darkness.

"Me, too, but it did."

"We should probably try to get more sleep."

Lucy chuckled before responding. "I agree with your idea but doubt I'll be able to make it a reality."

"Yeah, I was considering the same thing. It's still too early to get up though."

"Tell me about your favorite memory. Anything you want or think of that's a happy memory."

Just flipping through his happy memories was enough to help him relax and settle down. When he considered the time he asked his grandmother for macaroni and cheese, a smile broke through all his stress and worry.

"It was just after Nana came to get me from my mom. Neither of us really knew what to expect from the other or what the future would bring, but she wanted me to be happy. I was nervous about being away from what I knew as home, but her house was clean and comfortable. I could breathe and relax there."

Lucy hummed, and Jacks watched her shoulders relax more.

"I should mention that my grandmother had brought my dad over from Italy after her husband died. Her English was great, but she didn't always understand the American way of doing things, and goofy expressions like, 'Don't let the cat out of the bag,' would lead to her searching every bag in the house to try and find the poor, trapped cat."

Jacks chuckled and was thrilled to hear Lucy's giggle.

"Anyway, I was feeling homesick. Nana wanted to comfort me, so she offered to make me any food I wanted. When I'd lived with my mom, I'd eaten lots of Easy Mac. I could make it myself and having it in the house was a sign that my mom was doing well enough to grocery shop with me in mind. So that's what I asked Nana for. I wasn't surprised that she had no idea what it was, but her face lit up when I explained that it was just macaroni and cheese that went in the microwave. She looked so upset that she didn't have any, when she offered to make macaroni and cheese on the stove, I jumped on it. She shooed me away to watch cartoons while she cooked. I pictured her pulling out a blue and yellow box of Kraft, while I watched Looney Tunes.

It didn't take long for her to call me back out to the kitchen. There was a pot on the stove and a clean plate and fork beside it, but Nana looked concerned. She asked me if I was sure I didn't want anything else with it. I loved hot dogs with mac and cheese, but I knew we didn't have any, so I told her I was very excited just to have macaroni and cheese. She still looked worried, but she turned to the pot and started to scoop.

She piled angel hair pasta onto the plate and then piled freshly grated parmesan cheese on top."

Jacks had to stop talking for a minute as he laughed at the memory. He'd been so disappointed but didn't want Nana to know. Even as a child he'd recognized how much the meal represented her love for him, and there was no way he'd turn that down.

"She stared at me as I sat at the table to eat. She'd added butter to the noodles to keep them from sticking, and while it was nothing like yellow elbows, it was delicious. To this day, angel hair pasta with butter and parmesan is my go to comfort food."

"She sounds like an amazing woman," Lucy had completely relaxed and wiggled closer back into his arms. "I wish I could have met her."

"Me, too. Someday, I'll make Nana's macaroni and cheese for you."

"I'd be honored. It sounds delicious."

They continued swapping stories as the night wore on.

"My dad had this ongoing war with the local teenagers," Lucy said, laughing. "Every time he'd put up some fancy mailbox, they'd drive by with a baseball bat and smash it to pieces."

"Seriously?"

"Oh yeah. Finally he got fed up and installed this massive iron I-beam with a steel box, then encased the whole thing in bricks."

Jacks grinned. "That showed them."

"You'd think. One kid actually stuck a firework inside to try and blow it up."

"Did it work?"

"Blew the door clean off. But that was it." Lucy's eyes sparkled with mischief. "Dad was so smug. He replaced the door with this vinyl flap and stuck a teddy bear sticker on it—one making a very rude gesture."

"No way."

"Mom was mortified, but she refused to get involved in the mailbox wars. That sticker was still there when we moved to Tennessee."

Eventually, they saw the first glow on the horizon and emerged into the dawn to find a clear sky and no wind.

"Thank God," Lucy said, stretching. "No more rain."

Jacks checked his watch and winced. "We got maybe six hours of sleep. How long were you awake before you woke me?"

"Maybe an hour? It's hard to tell." She tested her jacket and sighed. "Still damp."

"Mine too. We'll have to hike in wet clothes." He began pulling their gear together, mentally cataloguing their remaining supplies. Two oatmeal packets, one tortilla, peanut butter, jerky, a protein bar, trail mix. Plus, they had coffee and cocoa.

"How's our food situation?" Lucy asked, as if reading his thoughts.

He held up the items one by one. "This is it. Enough for today if we're careful."

"And if we don't find the road today?"

Jacks met her eyes. "We need to find it today. Tomorrow morning at the latest."

She nodded, understanding the unspoken reality. Hell, Lucy probably understood better than him. Technically, they could survive a few days without food, but without the energy to hike out... he was counting on her navigation to save them sooner rather than later.

With that in mind he suggested, "I'm thinking we eat well this morning to make up for lack of sleep and get us off to a strong start."

Chapter 12

LUCY

Lucy studied the terrain ahead, trying to judge distances. One ridge west of the trail, she figured. The bear encounter pushed them further than expected yesterday. That was the one good thing that had come from their bear encounter. Well, that and the time she'd spent on Jacks' lap enjoying his kisses. The memory made her stomach flutter again.

"I'm not sure what you're thinking about, but I'm guessing it's more exciting than planning our path out of here." The grin on Jacks' face told her that he had a pretty good idea of her thoughts.

She smirked at him, "I started out thinking about distances and the map but got distracted by thoughts of your lap and your lips the second my mind conjured up the convergence of the streams." She wiggled her eyebrows in an exaggerated expression of her interest.

He laughed, "Come here."

She tried to saunter over to him in a sexy way but worried it might have looked stupid instead. Then she looked at his face as his smile shifted from humor to desire. He reached for her as soon as she was close enough to grab. Immediately, he wrapped one hand around the base of her skull and the other around her waist. Before his lips collided with hers, he whispered to her, "Is this what you were thinking about? Should we repeat the experience?"

When her brain became too tangled up with want to respond, he gently brushed his lips against hers just once before pulling back and offering, "Say the word, and I'll back off."

That got her functioning again. "Don't you fucking dare!" She rolled up onto her tiptoes, did her best to grab onto the short strands of his hair at the nape of his neck and licked his lips before nipping the bottom one with her teeth.

She felt a low chuckle rumble through his chest as he returned her passion. She happily made room for him to explore her mouth as she stepped close enough to be straddling one of his legs. His arm was so secure around her there was no fear of falling and she lifted herself higher up his thigh. He obliged her by bending his knee a bit more and lowering his arm to scoop down around her ass. Lucy's toes were still on the ground, but a good chunk of her weight was resting on Jacks' quad.

When she pulled back to breathe, she realized that she had been humping him. She expected to see an amused look on his face, but there wasn't even a hint of a grin. The only expression he wore was one of intense hunger. Lucy's breath hitched as she envisioned him laying her down, stripping off her clothes, and gifting her with waves of pleasure.

But even as desire coursed through her, a familiar ache bloomed in her chest. Not grief exactly, but something softer. A whisper of Ben's voice telling her she deserved to be happy, mixed with the strange guilt of feeling so alive when he never would again. The sensation didn't kill her want for Jacks, but it complicated it, layering her desire with an unexpected tenderness that made her eyes prick with unshed tears.

When she blinked, that vision of being with Jacks remained, but now it felt bittersweet. Beautiful and terrifying and weighted with the knowledge that loving someone meant risking loss all over again. Her arousal didn't vanish so much as transform, becoming something deeper and more fragile.

Jacks was still with her though. He didn't seem to have any trouble following her feelings. Slowly and gently, he straightened his leg and let her weight settle back onto her feet. He didn't pull back. His face relaxed into contentment, and he offered her gentle kisses across her nose and cheeks. He nibbled on her jaw playfully and relaxed his hands to settle around her ribs. His teasing released the sudden pressure she'd felt leaving her able to breathe again.

Soon, Lucy tucked her face into the crook of his neck and shoulder and whispered her apology.

Jacks jerked his head back away from her with a look of shock, "What? What do you mean? What are you sorry for?" She felt his fingers tighten into her skin. It wasn't painful, but she could tell he wasn't relaxed anymore.

"I didn't mean to get all complicated on you. I was enjoying it. I still am enjoying it. But then I started thinking about Ben and feeling guilty for not feeling guilty, if that makes any sense." She shrugged, feeling foolish. "I didn't mean to mess it up. It's just... this is all new territory for me."

Clearly, she was the most wishy-washy, flakey individual ever. Internally, she rolled her eyes at herself. He'd have to be nuts not be ready to walk away from her at this point. Just the other day, she'd been hiking along thinking that she was moving on and enjoying living her life again. Maybe she was further along than she'd thought, but apparently there were still layers to peel back.

She heard Jacks sigh as he dug his chin into the top of her head. "I want you to listen to me. I mean really hear me." He pulled back to look at her and check that he had her attention. Then he pulled her face to his chest so that she could hear his heartbeat while his voice reverberated through his chest.

"This is important, Lucy. We're under a lot of stress right now. We aren't eating as much as we should; we haven't slept as much as we should, you're injured, and we're hiking through much harder terrain than either of us are used to. Heck, if it weren't for your survival skills, I'd likely be sitting on a rock somewhere crying myself. I liked you before we ended up out here like this. I like you even more now. There is no reason to rush, nor should either of us expect this to be a simple path forward. Heck, you live in Tennessee, and I live in Pittsburgh. I'll understand if you decide to walk away," Jacks paused and his seriousness cracked before he continued, "Well, I'm hoping you'll at least lead me out of the woods before walking away."

Lucy couldn't help but giggle. She had no thoughts of abandoning him in the middle of a national forest.

"Anyway, I guess what I'm saying is I'm not going anywhere. How we go from here is up to you."

Lucy took a minute to process all of that while enjoying the steady rhythm of Jacks' chest. She wrapped her good arm around him and enjoyed the feeling of his fingers dancing along the back of her rib cage. She knew what she wanted. She also knew it was complicated.

JACKS

At first, when Lucy got quiet, Jacks feared the worst. In his mind, she was hugging him goodbye, and he started to prepare himself for losing her. But then her arm tightened around his back, and he felt the weight of her head settle into him. He realized that she was letting him support her while she thought. She might not even recognize how much she trusted him, but he knew. So even if she decided to walk away for now, he would accept it and give her time, but he wouldn't disappear. He would continue to stand there and support her until she was ready for him.

Then she spoke.

"I want to be with you. I miss Ben; I'll always miss him. He'll always be a part of me, but I'm still here. I still want to live. I want to get through this with you, and then I want to figure out things from there. But I want to do it all with you."

"I like that idea, and I would never expect you to forget about Ben. He had to have been a smart guy to have been with you."

"He was, but we should get going. Earlier, you started to say something about a big breakfast?" She looked skeptical.

"Yeah, but first I want to get a better idea of how far you think we are from the road."

Lucy stepped back. "I think we might be able to make it there today, but it would be late. If we don't hit the road by lunchtime tomorrow, we're more lost than I think." She looked nervous to even be saying that.

"Ok, so let's see if we can get there today. We'll have both packets of oatmeal for breakfast, split the bar for a snack, have peanut butter tortilla for lunch, jerky this afternoon or evening, and we'll hike hard to push for the road." He still wasn't sure how to handle reporting everything, but he wanted to get out of the woods.

"That sounds good to me," Lucy agreed.

Jacks left her to heat up water for their breakfast while he packed up everything else. Before long, he was holding the pot of oatmeal while they passed the spoon back and forth.

"You can tell me about Ben, you know." He didn't want to push her, but he was curious about the man she'd married. He'd noticed that she'd avoided telling stories about Ben earlier that morning.

"There's less to tell than you might think." Lucy paused to eat when Jacks handed her the spoon, but then she continued, "We were high school sweethearts and went to prom together. Then we went our separate ways and lost touch for a few years. I went home for the holidays my senior year of college and ran into him at the gas station. He invited me out to dinner to catch up, and" she shrugged, "we got engaged six months later."

Jacks finished the bite he'd just taken and handed her back the spoon. "How long did you say you were married?"

"He died just a couple months after our third anniversary."

There was a part of Jacks that was thrilled that Ben had died, and he felt like a complete shithead for it, but if Lucy were still married, there would be no place for him.

"It was a good three years, but it's also been nice to just be me again. I mean, I miss him, don't get me wrong, but it feels like we got married young. We were in our early twenties, but I feel like I've changed and grown up a lot since then." Lucy shrugged and scraped the last of the oatmeal from the pot. It appeared that was all she had to say about that. Jacks was hopeful she'd tell him more over time, but he wouldn't push.

"Here, I'll go rinse this, and then we can get going." Aside from their low food supply, he'd given Lucy the last of his Ibuprofen that morning. While it wasn't a strong painkiller, it was helping to keep the swelling from getting out of control and her pain manageable.

It didn't take long for them to return to the stream. Jacks insisted they take the opportunity to refill their water before continuing. Soon enough, they were back to trudging through underbrush and weaving between trees. A few times they arrived at the top of a rocky outcropping that required them to climb down, but none were overly difficult or dangerous. Without a pack to worry about, Lucy even managed to do alright with one arm in a sling.

The hearty breakfast helped to propel them forward, and Jacks pulled out the protein bar as soon as he noticed they were both starting to flag. Lucy had been leading them along at a brisk pace, and he was hopeful they'd be able to keep it up throughout the day. They stopped for a rest and lunch around noon, even if it just meant splitting one tortilla with peanut butter but got back to hiking with little fanfare. Both were aware that they had a clear goal of reaching the road. They didn't talk much, so they could focus their energy on making forward progress.

Even though they were hiking through the shade, by three pm they were feeling the heat of the afternoon sun. Jacks called for Lucy to find a place to take a break. They were able to relax on a flat rock that stretched out into the stream. Jacks insisted on massaging Lucy's calf, and they both drank their fill of water. Jacks tried to pull out the jerky, but Lucy wanted to save it for later. There was enough water now that the sound of it rushing past required them to speak up to hear each other.

In his head, Jacks was thinking about how long they should hike before stopping to set up camp for the night. He wanted them to go as far as possible, but he also wanted their tent set up before full darkness fell if they weren't going to be able to catch a ride tonight. They needed a good night's sleep, even if they got stuck spending it in the woods. He debated asking Lucy about it. He decided not to worry about it just yet. He could tell that she was preoccupied by pain but pushing through.

Sure enough, she didn't let them sit for long. They got up and back to hiking again but didn't get far before Lucy stopped suddenly.

"What's wrong"

"Shush a minute. Listen."

Jacks wasn't sure he'd been shushed by anyone since he was a child, but he trusted her, so he stopped to listen.

It took him a moment, but he did hear something. He just wasn't sure what it was. It did make Lucy smile, so he didn't think it was a bad thing.

She answered his unasked question, "I think it's cars."

He listened again. The sound wasn't always there, but every now and then, he'd hear a whoosh that sounded far off in the distance. It could be a car passing, but he wasn't sure and didn't want to get too excited.

Lucy, on the other hand, was bouncing on the balls of her feet. "Let's go! It has to be close."

If excitement helped override her pain, he was happy to indulge her. "Lead the way." He swept his arm forward and watched as she studied the woods to select their best path forward.

After another twenty minutes of hiking, Jacks was convinced they'd been wrong. He thought he might have heard the noise a few more times, but not enough to convince him a road was nearby. Lucy didn't seem at all discouraged and was still bouncing from tree to tree. He was debating if he should encourage her to save her energy when he heard the same sound, but much louder and clearly closer.

Lucy turned to grin at him, "I think that was a semi. We're almost there!"

And this time, Jacks was just as excited as she was. It wasn't even six o'clock yet, so they should be able to hitch a ride before dark, even. He stayed close on her heels until they could see light where the trees cleared ahead of them. A few more steps, and they caught site of the road just as a car went whizzing past. They had done it. Well, Lucy had done it. He felt his chest fill with pride and wanted to shout from the mountain tops that he had fallen for a girl who could find her way out of being lost in the woods. As soon as Jacks had the thought, he realized how true it was. He had fallen for her.

Chapter 13

LUCY

Never had she ever been so excited to see asphalt! There was a huge part of Lucy that had doubted she'd ever see anything beyond the forest again. She'd almost resigned herself to living the rest of her life lost in the woods with Jacks. She just wasn't willing to settle for only living a few more days or weeks. That was what had pushed her forward. It was more the thought of food than anything else that had led her onward.

Now that they had found civilization, she wasn't exactly sure what to do. Lucy had been so focused on getting this far, she hadn't considered what came next. They still had a couple of hours of sunlight, so walking down the road was an option. Her feet and legs weren't thrilled with the idea, but she could do it.

Even better was the realization that she could tell someone about the guns and Frank and everything else. Maybe it would make more sense to them. The exhaustion and pain were making it hard to think straight, but one thought kept circling through her mind: she couldn't be the only person to ever have trouble with them. In fact, it was likely they had a whole file about that chunk of the woods.

The more she thought about it, the angrier she became. Why hadn't this been shared with the hiking groups on Facebook or WhiteBlaze.net? Those were the two primary places hikers went for information, advice, to share memories, stay in touch with each other, and keep up with stuff like downed bridges, trail closures, and creepers.

Every step she took brought her closer to the road, and her anger built with each footfall. Her wrist throbbed in rhythm with her heartbeat, and the hunger gnawing at her stomach made everything feel more urgent, more unfair. How dare people keep stuff like this to themselves. For Pete's sake, she'd been drugged and dragged out into the woods to die like a lost hiker. Something had to be done to stop this nonsense.

Just as she realized that she was stomping more than stepping through the underbrush, she heard Jacks call for her to stop and wait for him. Lucy knew she wasn't thinking clearly, but the pain and exhaustion made it hard to care. She mentally rehearsed how she'd tell off whatever jerk of an officer thought it was more important to keep an investigation secret than share information that kept people safe.

"Being angry about finding the road that we've been looking for these last two days seems irrational to me. What's up?" he asked her with a raised eyebrow and note of skepticism in his voice.

Lucy's control was slipping. The constant ache in her wrist, the hollow feeling in her stomach, and the bone-deep tiredness were making everything feel impossible. "There's no way that we're the first people to have ever had issues along this part of the trail." She was literally tapping her foot in anger and frustration by this point, unable to stand still. "You can't tell me that the police around here don't have a file on this stuff, so why aren't they sharing it with the hiking community? Why isn't anyone posting about it on WhiteBlaze or Facebook? If they think that I'm going to just let it go because I want to keep moving along the trail, they've got another think coming. I will stay in this area as long as I need to, to press charges, testify, and make this crap stop."

Her voice was getting higher and shakier with each word. She had her good hand anchored on her outwardly jutting hip, and she could feel herself vibrating with an intensity that she knew wasn't entirely rational.

"Whoa! Okay, so I'm glad you're committed to stopping this. I am too, but I think we need to slow down and use some caution before just telling everyone all about it."

Lucy's eyes squinted into a tight, threatening glare, "Excuse me?"

Jacks just looked at her for a moment, and she could see concern creeping into his expression. The pause gave her time to remember that he wasn't the one who drugged her, nor had he been the one to leave her in the woods. He'd been on her side, helping her survive, keeping her as comfortable as possible, and taking care of her this whole time. Maybe he had something to say that was worth listening to. If nothing else, he'd probably earned the right to be heard.

In her head, she rolled her eyes at herself. There was no "probably." She needed to hear him out. He hadn't said anything foolish or stupid since his comments about the "property line," and he'd already apologized for that. Since then, he'd been nothing but respectful and supportive.

She stilled her feet and tucked her cocked hip back in line with her shoulders. She removed her hand from her hip and leveled her voice before prompting him, "What are you thinking?" Then she tried her hardest to stop thinking about all the ways she could harm someone who refused to share vital information and instead, focus on listening to what he had to say.

"I agree with the idea that local law enforcement must be aware of what's happening, but that might make the situation more dangerous. If they are involved or paid off to cover things up, going straight to them might not be our best idea. Remember how I said my friend Collin worked for the FBI down in Virginia?"

"Yeah," she really was listening to him now. He made a good point.

"I know I can trust him, so I was thinking we should get your wrist taken care of first, and then give him a call to get his advice. If nothing else, at least that way someone else knows where we are and what happened." He waited for her response.

Lucy deflated at the realization that he was completely right. If the cops were in on it, whatever "it" was, they were even more dangerous than Frank and his accomplices. The adrenaline that had been keeping her upright seemed to drain away all at once, leaving her feeling shaky and hollow.

"So, what do we do?" she asked him. "Are we better off walking down the road or waiting for someone to drive by?"

Her fleeting anger had taken her energy with it. She really wanted to lay down on the ground and go to sleep. The thought of people she'd always considered "good guys" working with the "bad guys" was more than she could deal with right then.

"Do you know which direction is Bennington?" Jacks asked her instead of proposing an answer.

Lucy took a minute to consider the map. She knew they'd hiked south, so they were on the north side of the road. She was confident that the trailhead was to the east. She thought Bennington would be to the west, but there was a chance they were already west of Bennington. When she said as much to Jacks, while pointing to the right, he seemed to study her for a few minutes.

"Let's have a seat here and enjoy the beef jerky and some trail mix. We'll consider our options as we watch how many vehicles drive past."

Lucy was beyond making decisions and shrugged in agreement.

The food certainly helped her feel better, and she perked up enough to feel like she could walk down the road a bit if they decided to do that, but she was still tired, and the pain in her wrist was quickly becoming bad enough to consume all her thoughts. It had now been more than eight hours since her last medication, and she was sure the swelling was getting worse.

They hadn't seen many cars drive past, and none of them had even slowed down when Jacks had tried to get their attention. Unfortunately, their seats under the trees hadn't allowed him to be visible to them until they were practically on top of him, so neither was surprised no one stopped. Lucy sighed her resignation to the inevitable, hauled herself off the ground, and got ready to start stepping down the road.

JACKS

Jacks stuck out his thumb as cars passed. It was not his favorite plan, but they needed to get Lucy medical attention.

"What if it's Frank?" Lucy asked, voicing his own fear.

"Then we run." He kept his thumb up as a Subaru approached. "But let's hope for the best."

The car slowed and pulled over ahead of them. Jacks tensed, knowing relief would have to wait until they were actually safe.

"I want to tell everyone what we found up there," Lucy said, shouldering her pack.

"I know you do. But we need to be careful." Jacks watched the Subaru's driver through the rear window. "Collin told me stories about small towns like this. Corrupt cops, criminals using locals to handle pieces of their business. Guns, drugs, worse things."

"You think they're all involved?"

"Maybe not all. But in a place this remote?" He gestured at the endless forest around them. "Everyone knows everyone's business. Could be they'd protect each other instead of helping outsiders like us."

Lucy's expression grew serious. "So what do we do?"

"Get your wrist looked at first. Then we'll figure out how to report what you found." He started toward the car. "Stay back with the pack while I talk to them, okay?"

She nodded, and Jacks approached the driver's side. Part of him feared it would be Frank, Grasshopper, or Tag-a-long, so when an older lady rolled down the window and hollered out, "Need a lift?" he was relieved.

"Yeah, is there a hospital nearby? My friend hurt her wrist, and I'm afraid it's broken." He nodded his head back toward Lucy, so the lady would know who he was talking about.

"Sorry to tell you the nearest hospital's a long way off. Good news is we got a clinic for urgent care stuff that's used to hiker injuries. They got x-rays and can fix up most stuff. It's about fifteen minutes away."

"Any chance you're going that way?" Jacks asked hopefully.

"Nope, but I didn't get milk this week, so I don't mind the detour back to town. Hop in."

Jacks waved Lucy over and they both climbed in the backseat with Jacks sitting behind the driver.

"I'm Betty, by the way." She looked at them in the rearview mirror and turned on her signal but made no move to pull back onto the road.

"I'm Logan, and this is Lucy." Jacks introduced them using their real names. He'd debated sticking with their trail names, but he wasn't sure Betty would understand "Loner," and if other craziness happened to them, he was hopeful she might prove to be good enough to report something. In which case, it might be good for her to know their real names.

Betty pulled out and made a U turn on the road to go back the way she'd been coming from. "I always appreciate when hikers use their real names. I understand the benefits of trail names, and some of them are fine, I suppose. There are others that just make me wonder, though. Who, in their right mind, agrees to answer to 'Gummy Saver' or 'Sockcap' or whatever other nonsense they come up with?"

Jacks chuckled and agreed with her as Lucy leaned her head on his shoulder. She'd put their pack at her feet and was gripping her forearm through the sling. He knew the pain had been bad since he'd run out of Ibuprofen for her. She rubbed her head on his shoulder, and he thought he might have heard a small whimper escape.

"How bad is she?" Betty dropped her boisterous volume to an almost discreet level as she asked him about Lucy.

"All things considered I think she'll be fine. I'll be shocked if the wrist isn't broken, but I think that's about it." He debated telling Betty about their whole adventure but decided not to for the time being.

"I noticed you weren't at the trail head. Been walking on the road for a bit?"

He couldn't help letting out a huff. He wished they'd just walked on the road after hiking down the trail. "No, you stopped just a few minutes after we found the road."

Betty's eyes snapped up to the rearview mirror before returning to the road. She drove silently for a few minutes before speaking again.

"You know this is a small community, right?"

"Yes, ma'am." Jacks felt like she was sharing important wisdom or secrets.

"I've been retired for a while now, but I taught around here for a long time. I got to know pretty much everyone in this area. Most all of them came through my classroom, including the local sheriff. He's a good man and honest. But I'd be lying if I said I wasn't surprised to see him in charge of the law around here. If you need to talk to him, you just let me know."

"I appreciate that." They were pulling into the urgent care place.

Before Jacks could open the door, Betty turned back over her seat and asked, "You have your phone handy? I can give you my number in case you need anything."

"No, ma'am. Both our phones are still back in the woods somewhere, we think." At least Jacks hoped their phones were lost somewhere in the woods. Until that moment, he hadn't even considered what it might mean if they had been picked up by Frank and his friends.

Betty dug around in her glove box and then her console before pulling up a paper napkin and pen. As she scribbled on the napkin, she told him, "Here's my number. You give me a call if you need anything. I'm putting George's number on here, too. He shuttles hikers to and from town all the time, so he usually knows what's going on along the trails."

Jacks accepted the napkin and folded it carefully before zipping it into one of his hip pockets. "Thank you. I'm sorry I don't have any money on me to give you right now."

"Here." Lucy chimed in for the first time as she handed Jacks a twenty she'd pulled from her pocket.

"How about you keep that in case you need it later. Maybe you can fill my gas tank the next time I give you a lift." The way she smiled at them led Jacks to believe that riding with her again would be as fortuitous as this first trip had been.

"Thank you, Betty. At the very least, I'll give you a call and fill you in on the details sometime," he promised her.

"I'd appreciate that. My life is far from boring, but I have a feeling your story would put most of mine to shame." She winked at him as he started to climb out while telling Lucy to stay put and let him come around.

He got the pack situated on his back before helping Lucy out and leading her into the clinic.

Chapter 14

LUCY

The clinic wasn't too busy at seven pm, so they got her x-rayed quickly. No one was surprised to see that her left wrist was broken. What was a surprise was that it wasn't misaligned, nor had it started to heal incorrectly. Even Jacks had been audibly shocked to find out there was no need for rebreaking, realignment, or surgery. Once they hooked her up with the good drugs, she'd been perturbed to learn that he'd expected her to get transferred to a hospital operating room but hadn't bothered to share that expectation with her.

Now, she was laying on a thin exam table and enjoying the floaty feeling that came with medication. She thought the people around her were talking about a cast or a brace or something about how to do something for her wrist, but she wasn't sure and couldn't find it in herself to care. What she wanted was food. She was hungry. A roast beef sandwich sounded amazing, or maybe pancakes with lots of butter and syrup. She wondered if she could convince Jacks they needed both. Plus, some crispy bacon and pineapple upside down cake would be great. Was that even something you could buy ready to eat or did you have to make your own?

Lucy tried to refocus on what was happening around her when she heard someone say her name. It looked like they were expecting her to respond.

"We should get lots of food," she told them.

When they laughed in response, she gave them her best wicked glare and imagined shooting lasers from her eyes. She'd buzz off the hair of the spikey-haired guy and zap the mole on the cheek of the blond lady.

"Ouch!" Her wrist didn't hurt the way it had, but when someone grabbed it and started moving it around, she could still feel the pain. She turned her laser eyes toward the young punk with spikey black hair and considered pulling her hand away from him. But that would take work, and she was tired. So, instead she started to imagine the perfect poofy cloud bed that would surround her with cushiony softness.

"You can lay back if you want." Were they talking to her?

Lucy felt Jacks' hand on her shoulder. She relaxed into him. She liked his hands. He helped her lay back on the crinkly paper. It made an annoying noise. Who thought it was a good idea to put paper on a bed? That was stupid.

And then he laughed!

JACKS

Lucy wasn't in pain anymore, thanks to whatever they'd given her. Jacks couldn't stop chuckling as random thoughts slipped from her mind straight out of her mouth.

"Food," she announced suddenly. "We need food. I'm starving. Are you starving?"

"Yeah, I'm hungry too." He squeezed her hand. "And I'm glad you're getting the removable cast instead of that plaster thing."

"It will be much better for hiking," she agreed drowsily.

When she dozed off, Jacks quietly stepped away from her bedside. He needed to make some calls, but he didn't want to leave her.

Greg appeared in the doorway, his spiky black hair making him look like a punk rocker despite his scrubs. "She doing okay?"

"Much better. Hey, could I borrow a phone? I need to call someone."

"Sure thing." Greg pulled out his cell. "It'll show up as a 757 number, since I'm not a local. You can use the consultation room next door if you want privacy." He handed over the device.

"Thanks, but I'd rather stay close to her." Jacks gestured toward Lucy. "How'd you end up here, if this isn't home?"

"I've got a traveling contract that has me here for the summer, when they need the extra help as hikers come through."

Jacks sighed with relief, feeling safer now that he knew Greg wouldn't have any connections to what was happening in the woods. "That's awesome, and thanks." He held up the phone.

Greg nodded. "Take your time."

He dialed directory assistance first. "FBI office, please."

From there, he was lucky enough to connect with someone who he'd met the last time he'd been visiting Collin. As soon as Jacks introduced himself as "Collin's friend, Logan," the guy had been happy to give him Collin's direct line.

"Special Agent Warner. How can I help you?" Collin sounded tired.

"Collin, it's me, Logan."

"Hey, man, what's up? My phone didn't recognize your number."

"Yeah, well, I'm not on my phone. I could really use your help."

"Wait, aren't you supposed to be out hiking this week?"

"There's where your help is needed."

"Oh, shit, are you okay? What's going on?" Jacks heard Collin's voice go from tired to friendly to professional. He could practically see Collin grabbing a notepad and pen just like he used to back in school anytime a teacher said something that interested him.

"I met a girl, but that's not the important part. It is, but it's more important that she found some guns and was then drugged and left in the woods to die. And when I ran into the same people, they threw hands, and I ended up high tailing it off the trail to get away. We don't know what's going on, but I think it's bad, and I'm worried that local law enforcement might be involved. At least, I have to imagine they're aware. In either case, I'm hesitant to go to them."

"Where are you right now?" Collin had shifted into full Special Agent Investigator mode.

"We're currently at an urgent care place outside of Bennington, Vermont. Lucy's wrist is broken, so we're getting that taken care of. My next plan is to get us a hotel for the night."

"Good. Pick a chain hotel and act like tourists. I'll be there tomorrow morning. Now explain the details, please."

"Dear God, you even sound like an FBI guy now!" Jacks couldn't resist busting his chops at least a little.

"That is why you called me." Jacks figured Quantico had to have included a class on how not to laugh no matter what your friend says based on the deadpan response Collin gave him. At the same time, he did appreciate having a friend who knew what he was doing with this situation.

"Fair enough." Jacks wasn't sure where to start the whole story. Should he start with Lucy finding the guns or explain how he met her. He didn't want to get sidetracked.

"So, you were hiking in Vermont. Did you start from Route Nine?" Professional Collin to the rescue.

"No. Work's been crappy recently, and I was aggravated by trying to schedule a shuttle. I decided to park at the Daniel Webster Memorial, head south to VT Nine, and then make the return hike. I didn't feel like climbing Stratton Mountain, but I wanted some time in the woods." Jacks could feel himself veering off track, so he refocused on the important parts of the story.

"I met Lucy just before I made the turn to go back north. We had lunch together and connected. I decided to make the turn quick, so I could catch back up to her. She was struggling with shin splints, so she was keeping her mileage slow and easy. Anyway, I figured I'd meet up with her somewhere between Goddard and Kid Gore shelters, but when I got to Goddard around lunch, all her stuff was there, and her tent was set up. But she was nowhere to be found.

"Instead, I met a guy named Frank and got into a fight with him and one of his buddies. Thanks for the fighting lessons, by the way. They saved my ass enough for me to get away. I ended up taking off into the woods. I thought I'd found a property line and started following it. It turned out to be pieces of Lucy's shirt that she'd tied to trees to leave a trail with the hope that someone would find her."

At this point, Jacks fully expected Collin to interrupt him with a comment about how he and Lucy had "connected" or at least to ask about how Lucy had ended up in the woods. But Collin just grunted at him to continue.

Jacks stuck to the basics as he filled in Collin. He tried his best to tell him the location of the guns, but he wasn't certain himself. Collin assured him that'd get more details from Lucy once he joined them.

By the time Greg appeared in the doorway wondering about his phone, Jacks was wrapping up his conversation and promising to text Collin which hotel he and Lucy would be staying at. He apologized to Greg for taking so long and offered to send him money to help with the bill, but Greg waved him off and assured him he had unlimited talk and text. He asked Jacks to just leave his phone at the main desk when he was done with it. Then he let Jacks know a nurse would be coming by soon with paperwork for Lucy before sending them on their way.

Once the door closed behind Greg, it only took Jacks a few minutes to get them a room at Best Western. Now, he just needed to figure out how to get them from here to there. It was after eight pm, in rural Vermont, on a Tuesday. He sighed and dug Betty's number out of his pocket.

Thank goodness for bored, little old ladies who like to help strangers. Jacks hung up with her just as one of the nurses came in with paperwork, instruction, and pain pills for later. He listened carefully and returned Greg's phone to the desk before waking Lucy as gently as he could and helping her out to the lobby. Betty pulled in just as they left the exam area, so he was able to tuck Lucy straight into the car.

"I can't thank you enough for the ride. I know it's late."

"Pshaw, don't think I won't charge you. I expect some excellent storytelling in exchange for my services. I'll be by with coffee and breakfast promptly at nine tomorrow morning, and I want to hear the whole adventure."

Who was Jacks to say no to that? He was very glad that she'd chosen a late morning time that would allow him and Lucy to get plenty of sleep. When he'd booked their room, he'd debated how many beds they needed. He really wanted her beside him, but he thought she might be comfortable with extra space, and he didn't want to presume anything. Then the desk clerk had informed him that they only had king rooms left, and the choice was taken out of his hands. Secretly, he had been thrilled by that development.

Jacks had asked Betty if she could drive thru a fast food place on the way to the hotel. She'd "pshaw" ed that also and promised she'd take care of it. He wasn't sure exactly what that meant and was a bit concerned when she drove them straight to the hotel. Given that she'd provided them with a free ride, he didn't want to pester her further and was hoping he could just order them a pizza or something once they got into the room.

He left Lucy in the car with Betty while he checked them in and got their room number. Betty was able to pull around to a side door that gave them closer access to their room, and he made sure she knew where to find them in the morning. He expected to grab his pack and Lucy before Betty drove away, but she surprised him by turning off the engine and climbing out with them. By this point, he was so tired, so hungry, so done with all of it that he really wanted to snap at her to just leave them alone so he could figure out food and get them settled.

Instead, he reminded himself how kind and helpful she'd been and slung his backpack on his shoulders before helping Lucy through the hotel door and down the hall. At least they were on the first floor, so he didn't have to deal with stairs or an elevator or anything.

The whole way down the hall, Lucy babbled about pancakes and burgers, and how much she loved him. He was trying hard to remember the drugs and ignore the last part. He worried that when she came back to her senses, she'd be weird about it or forget about it. There was also a tiny part of him that feared she'd remember saying it but regret it and take it back. He was trying to squash that part of himself down by his toes where he could pretend it didn't exist.

Eventually, he got them to their room and swiped his key card. Betty stepped in front of him and held the door open, so he could lead Lucy in. Then she surprised him again by lifting her own bag off her shoulders and setting it on the desk in the room.

"There's meatloaf, mashed sweet potatoes, green beans, apples, and brownies in there. I packed silverware for you, and I put each serving in its own container. I figured just eating out of those should be easier than trying to deal with plates. Oh, shoot, I left your waters in the car. I'll be right back" and off Betty jogged back down the hallway.

"Oh my goodness, meatloaf sounds amazing! Do you think she put sauce on it?!" Lucy was toddler level excited about the new development, and Jacks felt like an ungrateful asshole. He made mental note to learn about what Betty wanted or needed most in her life and provide it for her. He peeked in the bag to see very large containers of food for each of them along with a separate container of brownies with two huge, red apples on top of it. Betty chose that minute to pop back in through the door he'd propped open and caught him with his face buried in the bag.

"I tried to pack plenty. I know how hungry hikers get," she informed him as she placed four bottles of water on the desk with the food. "I'll be bringing pancakes for breakfast in the morning. I have some real maple syrup to go with, and Lucy seems rather keen on that idea."

Jacks was at a complete loss for words, so he walked over and hugged Betty.

"Thank you." It seemed inadequate, but he'd do his best to make it up to her later.

After closing the door behind Betty, Jacks turned to find Lucy already digging out silverware and opening containers.

She was completely earnest in her joy. The pain meds had wiped away any filters she would normally use to temper her responses, and Jacks loved it. They had been through hell, but they were both here, together, enjoying magnificent food and a comfortable bed.

Lucy's head began to bob before they opened the brownies, and the burning sensation in Jacks' eyes made it easy for him to follow her into bed. They still only had one set of clothes each, so he hung those in the bathroom and added a quick trip through Walmart to his plan for tomorrow. Then he wrapped his arms around the most amazing woman he'd ever met and drifted off to sleep.

Chapter 15

LUCY

It was the pain in her wrist that woke her, and she thought that was amazing. The previous few mornings she'd woken because of discomfort from sleeping on the ground, hunger pains in her empty stomach, muscle cramps from hiking too far with too little sustenance, and fear of being struck by lightning. Cracking her eyes open because the ache in her wrist was noticeable only happened because the rest of her was completely comfortable. The bed was soft, her belly was happy, and Jacks was warm. Though she should probably get used to using his real name now that they were back in civilization.

She vaguely remembered feelings of total joy and happiness last night. She might have even told Jacks, well Logan, that she loved him. As she snuggled back into Logan's warmth, she considered how she felt about that and quickly decided it had been an honest, if premature, statement. His arms tightened around her, and Lucy felt the cadence of his breath on the back of her neck change.

"Morning," Jacks' voice was still mumbly with sleep.

"Based on the one bed, I'm guessing your affection for me wasn't left in the woods." Lucy knew it was a heavy topic for first thing in the morning, but it was on her mind, and she needed the reassurance.

Jacks (nope, she had to think of him as Logan now) rubbed his nose below her ear before using his teeth to nip down her neck to her shoulder. She could feel just how "awake" he was this morning when he wiggled his hips against her ass.

"Yeah," he whispered in her ear, "I still love you."

Lucy rolled over and nuzzled her nose against his. "I love you, too. I meant it when I said it last night." She sealed the confession with a kiss and hoped he'd ignore her morning breath. What she really wanted was to take advantage of their nakedness and get to know him better but rolling over had shifted more pressure onto her wrist, and she needed pain meds first.

Apparently, Logan had noticed her wince. He reached over to the table beside the bed and picked up her prescription along with a bottle of water and handed them both to her.

"Let's start with this. Betty won't be back until nine, so we've got a little over two hours before we need to be presentable. Collin will also be here sometime this morning, but I have no idea when."

"How did you get ahold of him?" It dawned on Lucy that neither of them had a phone.

"Greg, the guy at the clinic with spikey hair, which you kept threatening to buzz, was nice enough to let me borrow his. I did have the forethought to write down Collin's number, though, so I might be able to give him a call from another phone." Jacks looked over at phone on the desk thoughtfully.

"We'd need a phone card, or something, wouldn't we? Is long distance still a thing?" she wondered.

"I was just wondering the same thing. You drink some water and take a pill, while I hit the restroom and try making a call. We'll reconvene here in bed in just a few minutes."

Lucy smiled, inhaled, frowned, and added, "I think I need to put a shower somewhere on that list, Logan." She added his name just to test it out on her tongue, but the way his face lit up confirmed it for her. She'd met a hiker named Jacks but fallen in love with a man named Logan who wasn't great at finding his way around in the woods but knew exactly what she needed from him.

"I like the way you say my name, Lucy." He was all out flirting with her now. "Should we change our meet up point to the shower?" he asked with a bit of teasing in his voice.

Lucy liked the way Logan said her name too, and the thought of his hands being the ones to rub her skin clean sounded like heaven. She wasn't discounting the thrill of being able to touch him everywhere either.

She pulled herself up to a seated position with her back leaned against the headboard while Logan sauntered off to the bathroom. There were only five pills in her prescription bottle, but considering they were Percocet, she was hoping to switch to over-the-counter meds even before taking all five.

As she listened to Logan flush and wash his hands, she tried to remember what all he'd told her about Collin. She remembered the two of them had gone to high school together and been best friends. She was thinking that Collin had been Logan's one friend to complete the AT the year that he'd tried to thru hike it. And, she remembered that he worked for the FBI. Didn't stuff have to cross a state line before the FBI could get involved? She couldn't remember. In any case, it was reassuring to have someone to help them figure out what to do from here.

When Logan emerged from the bathroom, Lucy took her own turn. She remembered the uneaten apples as she was drying her hands and decided that would be the perfect morning snack.

She found Logan on the phone with Collin when she came out to dig through the bag Betty had left with them. The apples were as big and shiny as she remembered, which surprised her because most of her memory of the night before was a bit fuzzy. In any case, she savored the crisp crack as the first bite of apple broke free and oozed juice down her chin. It was as delicious as it looked.

Lucy heard Logan say, "Yeah, Best Western room one fifteen. We'll see you around ten. I have to go now," before he abruptly hung up the phone while staring at her the same way she'd been staring at the apple.

"Did you end up having to call collect?" she tried to ask through her full mouth. She also wanted to wipe her chin, but the brace didn't make that easy. She didn't see any napkins or paper towels.

Logan licked the juice from her chin up to her lips and ended all her thoughts about collect calls, apples, and wrist braces.

"We should go get that shower now," Logan's voice rumbled deep in his chest as he took the apple from her hand and set it on the desk before continuing to kiss her while walking her backward into the bathroom.

He pulled away to close the door but stopped. "Are you okay with this?"

She loved that he took the time to check in. "Yes, I want us to both get clean, and then I want you to take me to bed. Naked. Together." She didn't want any misunderstandings or for him to hesitate anymore. She would have suggested they do it in the shower, but she already had one broken wrist and didn't feel the need to push her luck.

"Good." Logans shoved his shorts down his legs and nodded at her underwear, "You don't need those."

Lucy was happy to oblige him.

"The doc said you can remove the brace only long enough to shower, but you can't move your wrist or use your hand for anything. Let's take it off, but then I'm in charge of cleaning both of us. You're in charge of keeping that arm still." She loved his confidence in that moment and grinned as she nodded at him.

Logan unstrapped the brace while holding her hand steady. She used the time to admire his scruffy jawline, the slight bump in his nose, and the crinkles beside his eyes. She knew he was in his early thirties, which put him about half a decade ahead of her. In her mind, it was perfect. They both had enough experience to be confident in who they were and what they wanted, but neither was old enough to be completely cynical and jaded.

Logan stepped into the shower and adjusted the water to a reasonable temperature before holding out his hand to steady her as she stepped over the edge of the tub. When she started to reach for the soap, he glared at her until she pulled her right hand back and used it to steady and support her left. Then she stood there while he poured shampoo into his hands, soaped up her hair and rubbed down her entire body.

He didn't waste any time before rinsing her off, though he did massage her scalp while rinsing her hair. Logan seemed to agree that the shower wasn't the best place for them to get sexy. He helped her out, dried her off, and put the brace back on her wrist before climbing back in to wash himself.

"Stay right there. I'll only be a minute," he even winked before closing the curtain. She took the opportunity to use one of the two toothbrushes Logan had gotten from the front desk when he'd checked them in. She hadn't even finished rinsing her mouth when she felt Logan's wet arms wrap around her. She wiggled and squirmed and complained about how wet he was while he laughed and shook his head to spray water all around the room.

Both of their demeanors changed as Logan shifted his hands to tweak her nipples and cup her breasts. His lips ghosted across her ear, "We should move to the bed. Go lie flat on your back in the center of the bed. I want to taste you."

LOGAN

"

JACKS

"

MILLER

He loved how strong Lucy was and appreciated the way she'd been able to lead them through and out of the wilderness. She was clearly used to handling situations herself and taking responsibility for whatever might need to be done. He loved that about her, but he also wanted to give her a place where she didn't have to worry about anything. When they were in bed together, he wanted to take charge of spoiling her, pleasing her, and pushing her to forget everything but this moment between them.

Lucy pulled her feet up flat onto the bed to give him access to her center, but that wasn't where he planned to start. He wanted to taste all of her. Logan lifted her left foot first and worked his way slowly up her leg before doing the same with her right leg. Then he used his tongue to explore her hip bones. By the time he got to her navel, she was squirming and begging him for more while trying to use his hair to tug him in the direction she wanted him to go.

He kissed her intimately just once as he shifted up onto his knees and straddled her waist. He leaned over and tangled his fingers through her hair before aligning his lips with hers. "Will you be patient for me," he ghosted his soft request across her mouth before adding, "This is my first time getting to properly appreciate your entire body. I promise I won't deny you anything, but I'd like to take my time getting there."

Lucy's eyes widened and she nodded her agreement.

"Thank you." He rewarded her with another kiss before moving her left arm out to lay beside them on the bed. "Keep that arm there, so I don't have to worry about hurting it."

She just nodded again, and he returned to his exploration by picking up where he'd left off at her rib cage.

By the time he had made it all the way up to her face, he'd learned that she was ticklish in several places, and the sides of her neck were the secret controls to her hip movements. He moved much quicker as he made his way back down between her legs and ensured that her patience paid off. Based on the lazy smile and limp limbs he saw when she was finished, she didn't have any regrets.

He had one, though. He didn't have a condom with him. They were both responsible adults, and it didn't sound like she'd been sleeping around, so he wouldn't mind going without. He wasn't sure how she felt about it, though, and would respect her wishes.

"I haven't been with anyone since Ben died," she confessed when he crawled up beside her and asked for her thoughts.

"It's been about six months for me, but that had been a one night stand, so I've been tested since then."

Lucy leaned up to kiss his cheek before replying, "I'd like to think we'll last more than one night, and I trust you, so I'm okay without one. I'm on birth control, so there's no worries there."

Logan's brain shut down the moment she'd agreed to go without a condom. There were no words left for him to say other than that he loved her. So, he told her that while anchoring himself between her thighs and watching her face shift with pleasure as they united. He was carefully to let her lead them down the rabbit hole but blissfully followed right behind her.

He leaned to her right side as he collapsed onto the bed and pulled her onto his chest. She just hummed, and they both drifted contentedly while he trailed his fingers up and down her back and she swirled circles through his chest hair.

Lucy pressed a soft kiss to his sternum before looking up at him. For the first time since Ben's death, she felt completely, utterly alive. Not just surviving, not just moving forward, but truly living again. The realization settled into her bones like warmth from the sun.

Eventually, he extracted himself from their bubble long enough to look at the clock. They had about forty-five minutes before Betty would arrive. He didn't want to disturb Lucy, but he also wasn't willing to risk them still being naked when Betty came knocking. Which led him to consider clothing and realize that they had nothing but the gross, dirty hiking clothes they'd both been wearing for several days now. He had intended to ask Collin to pick them up something on his way in, since he was driving from Virginia. Seeing the juice from the apple trail its way down Lucy's chin while her eyes rolled in pleasure had distracted him. Even thinking about it had him wondering if they had time for another round.

He noticed that Lucy's circles had trailed down far enough to hint that she might be thinking the same, so he pulled her up to straddle him and offered to take her for a ride. She giggled and agreed. From there, they didn't waste any time and were soon back in the shower together for a quick clean up. Logan had Lucy keep the brace on this time and just had her hold her arm up in the air while he washed her quickly before doing the same for himself.

As they wrapped themselves in towels, he confessed that he wasn't sure what they should do for clothes.

"Call Betty. You know she'll pick stuff up for us. I have some extra cash buried in my pack..." Lucy stopped suddenly and looked heartbroken. "Never mind."

"No, I think you're right. I'll call Betty. I want to be sure to pay her back for the food and rides anyway. Maybe we can do something nice for her once things settle down."

"We should definitely come back to visit. I got the impression she'd like the company."

"I was thinking the same thing." Logan was glad to see Lucy smile again, even if it wasn't quite as bright as before.

It didn't take him long to reach Betty. There wasn't anywhere convenient for her to stop, but she was happy to bring some of her late husband's things along with an extra outfit of her own for Lucy. Logan imagined he might end up in a weird, blue, velvet leisure suit, but it would give them something to wear while they ate. He went ahead and called Collin back about picking up several new outfits for them, even though it meant enduring Collin's teasing about the abrupt way he'd ended their previous call. Collin had been right to note that Logan was much happier and more relaxed now, though, so he couldn't really be upset with his friend.

Lucy and Logan scrolled through the TV stations while wrapped in towels until Betty arrived. She brought a casual dress for Lucy that was cut in way that made it look perfect for her, even though it might not have been her exact size. For Logan, he was thrilled to find a pair of chino work pants and a button up shirt. The shirt was a bit small, but the pants fit well enough. The waistband was too big, so they hung very low on his hips. When he saw Lucy eyeing the V that they exposed, he decided the pants were the ideal size.

Betty brought enough pancakes and sausage for all three of them and stayed to join their meal. They ended up having just enough time to eat, chat, and clear the desk before Collin knocked on the door. Once Lucy and Logan had explained to Betty that they'd need to share the whole story with Collin, she been happy to wait and hear it at the same time. She was also relieved that they were calling in outside help.

She'd ended up confessing that she'd taught the local sheriff, "Mikey," and she wasn't impressed by him. He was older now. He'd been one of her first students back when she was a young high school teacher, but he hadn't seemed to get much smarter with age. She assured them that it wasn't likely he was involved with anything bad, but she also wasn't confident that he'd do anything helpful.

The three of them invited Collin into the room, but he pointed out how crowded it was and returned to the front desk to get access to a conference room. Based on the way he'd scrunched up his nose, Logan realized the smell of sex might also be lingering beneath the odor of pancakes and sausage. He hadn't even thought about it before inviting Betty in. He and Lucy had tossed the cover up over the bed, but that had been about it. Betty hadn't batted an eye or made a single comment, but then she might just be more restrained and polite than Logan's best friend.

Chapter 16

LUCY

Collin wasn't what Lucy expected. Logan was tall and broad-shouldered, but he was lean enough for his muscles to be well-defined. Collin was built more like a tank, or perhaps a linebacker. His shoulders were large enough to shrink his neck, and there wasn't a soft spot anywhere on him. He was wearing the traditional, dark, FBI suit, but Lucy wasn't sure how he managed to find a jacket that fit over his arms and still allowed him enough range of motion to pull a gun.

"Lucy," Logan had caught her staring, "let's sit down, so we can explain everything." He looked concerned by Lucy's focus on Collin, so she sat right next to him and put her hand on his leg. Collin sparked her curiosity, but that was it. Perhaps his suit jacket had some spandex woven into it to allow enough stretch for him to move freely. That would be crazy smart!

"Ahem," Collin cleared his throat and looked back and forth between her and Logan.

"Does your jacket stretch?" she blurted out. She was already making a fool of herself by being so distracted, she might as well satisfy her curiosity so she could focus.

Both Collin and Logan laughed, but Collin did answer her. "No, but I do have my suits custom made to ensure I can do my job."

"She just took a pain pill with breakfast," Logan commented to Collin. At first, she thought it was random, but then she considered it might be impacting her attention.

In any case, it was time she started telling her story. Betty was lounging at one end of the conference table while she and Logan rolled their chairs up against each other on one side and Collin sat on the other side facing them. Betty had promised she'd only observe and listen. While they all knew her primary interest was in the hot gossip, Collin had also mentioned her local knowledge could be helpful.

Everyone, including Logan, listened intently while she explained her entire experience. Occasionally Logan would rub her shoulder where he had his arm stretched across the back of her chair, and Collin was writing furiously on his notepad, but no one interrupted her. She had paused when she described reconnecting with Logan after he scared her senseless, but Collin had nodded for her to continue and mentioned that Logan would tell his story after she'd finished.

She expected him to have questions once she finished, but instead he looked at Logan, "Normally, you two wouldn't be allowed to hear each other's statements, but right now I'm only here in an unofficial capacity. For now, I'm going to save my questions. If this turns into an official investigation, we'll go from there." Then he nodded at Logan, "Start with your northbound hike."

Logan did exactly that, but when he was done, Collin looked more perplexed than anything. "How confident are you the flowers weren't marijuana?" he asked Logan.

Lucy jumped in, "They had wide, flat petals and were arranged as single flowers not groups of tiny blooms. They were also more of a dark, royal purple."

"She described them better than I could have," Logan added.

"Fair enough." Collin sat and thought for a minute.

"Tell me about the local sheriff." He turned his attention to Betty.

"That's Mikey. He's in his early fifties now and has been sheriff for more than a decade. He's not the brightest bulb in the box, but he's a good person who wants to do right by his people. He just doesn't always know what "right" is, and he can't always understand what's going on right in front of him."

"Can we trust him to run this investigation?" Collin asked bluntly.

Betty thought about it for a minute before responding, "We can trust him to ask around and look into things, but if the people involved really are local, there's a good chance he's related to them, or at least knows them. It wouldn't take much for him to believe anything they tell him."

Now, it was Collin's turn to think. Lucy's eyes were feeling heavy. The pain pill she'd taken that morning wasn't nearly as mind-warping as what they'd given her at the clinic the day before, but it was still packing enough of a wallop for her to be ready for a nap. She leaned her head on Logan's shoulder and felt his arm wrap snugly around her shoulder.

"We need to at least try working with the sheriff. I can take over if I have to, but it would be better to have local law enforcement start the investigation. Do you have his number?" Collin looked at Betty.

"Nope, but I know people who do." Betty pulled out her phone and started tapping on the screen. A few minutes later, she looked back up and read off a string of ten numbers.

"Normally, I'd say that Lucy should make this call, but she looks more asleep than awake." Lucy nodded in agreement without lifting her head from Logan's shoulder. "In this case, you should call, Logan," he continued.

Lucy's brain knew that Collin was right. She understood that it needed to be reported, and that she and Logan needed to be the ones to make the report. But the rest of her really wanted to curl up in a soft, warm bed with Logan, lick her wounds, and ignore the world for at least a week. She sighed deeply before allowing her brain to mentally scold the rest of her. Then she lifted her head and prepared to do what needed to be done.

"I can make the call, Logan. I'm the one who found the guns."

"Are you sure?" Logan had already pulled out the cheap phone that Collin had picked up for them and was starting to dial. He studied her without hitting send. "We could at least wait until later. You could take a nap first."

"Logan," Collin stopped him, "you know the call needs to be made sooner rather than later. You've already been off the trail for more than twelve hours. Waiting until morning makes sense; waiting longer will be hard to explain."

Logan glared back at Collin, "You do understand that we're the victims, right? We didn't do anything wrong."

"Which is exactly why we need to make it easy and simple for the sheriff to focus on investigating others without wasting time looking into the two of you." Collin raised his eyebrows as a challenge to Logan to contradict him.

Lucy decided that it would be easier to just get things rolling, so she snatched the phone from Logan and hit send.

She did click the speaker button, so that everyone would be able to hear. That had the fortunate side effect of forcing Logan and Collin to stop bickering aloud. They were still giving each other a variety of meaningful looks, but their conversation had been put on mute.

"Sheriff's Office, this is Carla." The voice sounded like someone who was more deeply involved in other work and was perfunctorily answering the phone.

"Hi. Um, I found a bunch of guns buried in the woods and some people took me from my tent in the middle of the night and dropped me off somewhere in the woods." Lucy felt exceptionally stupid phrasing it like that, but when she'd considered saying that she'd seen guns and then been drugged, kidnapped, and left to die, her lungs had seized up and forgotten how to do their job. She was hoping to work up to the full severity of the situation gradually.

"Uh huh, and who would you like to speak with about that?" Carla asked distractedly.

Lucy felt her frustration building. "I was drugged and left to die by people hiding lots of big, scary guns. I want to talk to the police," Lucy blurted before Logan could jump into the conversation.

The other end of the phone line went silent before Carla asked, "Did you say you took drugs and almost died?"

This time Lucy just handed the phone to Logan while Collin pinched the bridge of his nose.

LOGAN

"No, she most certainly did not. What she said was that three criminals drugged her, knocked her unconscious and dragged her body off into the woods expecting her to die there. Luckily, she's a survivor. Also, she found a stash of automatic weapons hidden in a way that leads us to think it might be connected to her being dragged from her tent in the middle of the night. So, she needs to give a statement, or make a report, or whatever, to the sheriff or a deputy because someone Tried. To. Kill. Her." Logan kept his voice level, though he wanted to throttle whoever this incompetent person was.

"Hold on a moment please." Logan could hear Carla passing the phone off to someone else.

"This is Sheriff Michael Clark. How can I help you?" He sounded much more alert and attentive, and Betty nodded at Logan to signal that he was speaking to the man himself.

"Yes, sir. My name is Logan Miller, and I'm here with my significant other, Lucy Graves. We've been hiking along the Appalachian Trail but ran into some trouble. Lucy discovered a cache of hidden weapons. When she stopped for the night, she was drugged and left in the woods to die. I intended to catch up with her the next day and found her things but not her. I believe I ran into the people who hurt her. They tried to attack me, but I was able to fight them off long enough to get away. Unfortunately, I ended up wandering around lost in the woods myself. Luckily, Lucy and I found each other and managed to bushwhack our way down to VT Nine." Logan wasn't sure how long he'd have the sheriff's attention, so he wanted to make the most of it while he could.

"That does sound like a bit of trouble. Why am I not hearing about this from Lucy?" he didn't exactly sound accusatory, so Logan tried to focus on the fact that he was listening, rather than losing his patience with the sheriff.

"She's the one who called, but when Carla didn't seem to understand, I jumped in to try and help explain things. We took Lucy to the urgent care clinic in Bennington as soon as we caught a ride last night. Her wrist is broken, so they prescribed pain medication for her."

"Alright. Can you both come into the station to make your report, or do you need me to come to you?" Logan was relieved. The sheriff was listening.

"We can come to you, but we'll have the people giving us a ride with us." Logan wasn't about to leave Betty out. She seemed thrilled by the whole adventure and had done so much for them. He also wanted Collin there in case they needed his help or support with anything.

"Hmm, who're you getting a ride from?" Sheriff Clark's voice contained nothing but curiosity. Betty jumped in before Logan could respond.

"Hi, Mikey. It's just me and a friend of mine who's visiting for a bit. I'll bring Lucy and Logan to your office in about a half hour. Collin and I will hang out and eavesdrop while you talk to them." Betty was grinning with glee.

Logan could practically hear the sheriff rolling his eyes through the phone as he answered her, "Mrs. Sanderson, I'm glad to hear you're doing well and always appreciate you helping out in the community, but you really don't need stick around. You and your friend should go enjoy yourselves. I'll take care of the two hikers." He suddenly sounded painfully kind and overly professional.

"Nonsense! You know staying on top of what's happening is one of the things I miss most since I retired. This is the perfect opportunity for me to learn more about what's going on around here. We'll see you soon, Mikey." Logan was still holding the phone, so he didn't end the call as quickly as he suspected Betty would've liked him to.

"Please call me Sheriff Clark, or at least Michael, Mrs. Sanderson. I haven't been Mikey for many years now."

"My apologies, Sheriff. See you soon," Betty nodded at Logan who was ready for the quick disconnection this time.

Collin had been taking notes through the entire conversation. As he finished, he looked up, "Thank you for introducing me as your friend. I can show my badge, if necessary, but it would be best to avoid it or at least wait as long as possible."

"Oh, it's my pleasure. Did you get a room here, too?"

"Yes, ma'am. I'm up on the second floor."

"Good. We'll leave your car here and just take mine. We should get going. Lucy can nap in the car."

She'd been leaning heavily on Logan throughout the phone call. He knew she wasn't asleep, but she wasn't far from it. He made eye contact with Collin, who silently agreed to sit up front and chat with Betty.

Lucy's twenty-minute power nap on the drive seemed to revive her. Logan was glad to see her eyes were bright, and she appeared to be feeling well.

"How's your wrist?"

"It's good. I can still feel it, but it doesn't really hurt. It's more like an occasional throb, like a dull start to a headache but in my wrist."

"Good. Let me know if you need more pain killers," he didn't want her to wait until the pain was awful before taking her meds.

"Don't worry, I will. I do want to switch to Ibuprofen, though. I don't like the strong ones." Lucy's face wrinkled up.

Logan hadn't even thought about how they might remind her of how she felt waking up in the woods after being drugged. He took a moment to look at her more closely, but she didn't seem really bothered. They needed to follow Collin and Betty inside, so it was best to leave his worries behind for now. He could ask her about it later.

The sheriff's office was just one corner of a small, single story brick building that appeared to house several county offices. The building was accessible from all four sides, and it looked like each one was dedicated to something different. They had parked in front of the library but saw the sign for the sheriff's office hanging above the door just around the corner.

When Logan and Lucy caught up to Betty and Collin, he could hear Betty explaining that the nine, one, one dispatch office was on the far side of the building and the county health office was on the other side of the library. Collin appeared much less surprised by this setup than Logan was. When he looked over at Lucy, she was nodding her head as if it made complete sense, so it must be a rural thing.

As soon as they stepped through the door, an oversized woman with wild red hair looked up, huffed, and greeted them by saying, "The sheriff will be with you shortly. Just have a seat there," as she pointed her pen at a few chairs lining the wall of the entry. Then she returned to her word search.

"Good morning to you, too, Carla. Such a pleasure to see you. How is your family?" Betty asked her with such a false sense of cheer, Logan had to stifle his snicker.

Carla's pen didn't move. Her hair didn't move. Nothing moved except her eyeballs, which shifted focus away from the page in front of her to glare at Betty.

"Oh, that's right dear. My old brain had completely forgotten. I was so sorry to hear that Barry left you and took Junior with him."

Logan turned himself around to face the wall and tried to prevent his shoulders from shaking. Betty hadn't forgotten. Betty was wicked in the best kind of way. The anger and frustration that Logan had felt at Carla's response to Lucy on the phone had been completely avenged. Betty might just replace Collin as his new best friend.

Sheriff Clark appeared before any of them had time to sit. As he ushered them back to a conference room, he apologized for Carla while commenting that she had been struggling since Barry left. Logan suddenly felt bad and wondered if Betty's comment hadn't been too much.

Then Betty chimed in, "You'd think after six years, we'd all be allowed to move on. For heaven's sake, Junior's got his own apartment now and works at the library right here in this building," and Logan's guilt vanished. "Really, Mikey, you need to tell her to get over it or get a new job. When someone needs to report a problem, they should not have to contend with her nonsense." She sounded exactly like a teacher scolding their student.

"You're never going to call me Michael, let alone Sheriff Clark, are you, Mrs. Sanderson?" He seemed resigned to this fate.

"You're old enough now, it's easy to forget that you can still learn new things. I call you Mikey to remind you of that. Hopefully, it also reminds you of all the stupid things that children are capable of that should not doom them for life." At this, she raised an eyebrow at him.

"Yes, ma'am." His soft smile suggested that he knew exactly what she was talking about. "Alright, come have a seat and let's get started. Anyone need coffee or anything?"

They all declined his offer and quickly settled themselves around the rectangular table. For some reason, Logan had expected them to be separated or put in an interrogation room like he'd seen on TV. Collin didn't look at all surprised by the conference room, so he figured it was a TV thing. Whatever the case, he was happy to be able to sit next to Lucy.

She wasn't leaning on his shoulder, nor did she put her hand on his leg. She sat up straight, tall, and proud. She looked gorgeous.

Chapter 17

LUCY

The dynamics between these people reminded Lucy of the small town she'd grown up in. Before she and her parents had moved to Tennessee, when she was starting high school, she'd lived in rural Ohio. The community had corn fields instead of forests and flat forever roads that allowed a person to see clear to eternity instead of winding veins of travel climbing up, over, and around mountains, but had otherwise been very similar to this one. She remembered that the library she'd visited as a child had also shared space with the county health center. Her mother had bribed her to get her shots by letting her pick out books afterward.

Based on Logan's expressions, she figured he had some concerns about this sheriff's professionalism, or lack thereof.

Given her experience, she knew his competence could go either way, but his knowledge of the local area and people would be unmatched. She also knew it would be tough for him to listen to and trust a random stranger over people he'd known his whole life. Especially since those were the people who voted him into office. So, she needed to put her best foot forward.

"It's a pleasure to meet you, Sheriff Clark. Your community is lovely, and if the rest of your people are anything like Betty, they are wonderful, too." She caught Collin's smile and nod. She was on the right track.

"Why thank you. We get lots of hikers and tourists coming through and try to always be hospitable."

"After everything that's happened recently, I'm certainly glad you're here and so committed to everyone's safety."

"Yes, what exactly has happened?" He pulled out his phone and tapped the screen a few times before asking, "Do you mind if I record this?"

"Of course not."

"Let's start with your name and where you're from."

So, she did. And then she went on to tell him about stepping off the trail to dig a cathole only to find a stash of guns, meeting Frank, and setting up camp alongside Grasshopper and Tag-a-long.

As she told her story, he stopped her occasionally to ask questions or clarify something. He jotted down a few notes, especially her response to his questions, but otherwise he let her talk.

She explained waking up in the woods with a headache and shredding her shirt to leave a trail. In hindsight, she was very glad to have done that. Assuming the scraps were still tied to the trees it would make it much easier to show exactly where they had been.

When she got to the part about Logan showing up, he'd given her a very skeptical look. She'd felt Logan sit forward at that point and start to explain how he'd followed her trail of shirt scraps. Sheriff Clark opened his mouth to stop Logan, but Betty stopped him.

"Let him fill in the story as they go."

He looked at her for a moment but relented and nodded at Logan to go ahead.

Lucy was impressed by the way Logan freely admitted that she'd schooled him on the difference between property line markers and the trail she was leaving. He was also able to explain the way she'd gotten them to water. Given her pain, exhaustion, and hunger at the time, her recollection was hazier than his. He was able to recall details that she'd been completely unaware of.

When they'd finished telling the entire story and answered all of Sheriff Clark's questions, he leaned back and looked at them for a moment.

"I know Frank. He's a local boy."

Betty had visibly recoiled when Lucy had spoken about meeting him, so she wasn't surprised to hear this.

"He's not the sharpest tool in the shed, but he usually doesn't mean no harm. Tag-a-long might well be his younger brother, Jacob. They can both usually be found over at the general store. Any chance you'd be willing to go that way and see if you spot them and can confirm it's them? My niece works there and makes the best tea you'll ever have. Even if we don't find the boys there, the trip will be worthwhile."

"I've heard about the new tea she's been brewing recently but haven't had a chance to try it myself. Why don't I drive them over there?" Betty suggested.

"Sorry, Mrs. Sanderson, but I need to drive Logan and Lucy over myself. You and Collin are welcome to do as you please. Her tea is wonderful, but there's no need for you to join us if you have other things to tend to."

"We'll follow you there," Betty said with a dismissive wave.

It wasn't a long drive, but the sheriff chatted the whole way. Apparently, his niece, Jenn, was his family's pride and joy. She'd been working at the store since graduating high school. The owner had recently allowed her to add a small cafe like counter where she'd quickly become locally famous for her hot tea. Sheriff Clark went on about how she was hoping to open her own shop in the next couple of years and what a great mind for business she had. She sourced everything local and even grew some of her own ingredients.

The building they parked in front of looked like a giant barn but had a "GENERAL STORE" sign hanging on the front of it. The door was like the front door of a normal house. The top half was a window, but the bottom was solid door. It even had a standard doorknob with a slot for a regular key. There had been windows installed along the front of the building, so Lucy could see that there were shelves of goods like a convenience store.

Betty pulled in right behind them, and Collin hopped out before any of them made it to the door. He was clearly unwilling to miss any of this. It was the first time that Lucy felt like they weren't doing things in a way that Collin was used to. It made her nervous, but the thought of a cup of delicious hot tea overpowered those concerns. She was confident that Collin and Logan would keep them safe if they did run into Frank and Tag-a-long, or Jacob. It was odd for her to think of him as anything other than "Tag-a-long," but then it had taken effort for her to shift to thinking of Jacks as Logan.

Sheriff Clark held the door open for all of them, but Collin pushed his way forward to be the first to enter. Lucy noticed the discreet way he checked for his gun in his shoulder holster before crossing the threshold. She followed him with Logan right behind her and Betty bringing up the rear.

They all filed toward the counter along part of the back wall. There was an open doorway behind the counter that led to a storage area. Lucy could see boxes stacked back there. There were no stools along the counter, but then there wasn't really room for any. It was obvious the shelves had been squished closer together to make room for the counter rather than eliminating any display space. Anyone who doubted only had to look at the rusty marks on the floor to see where the shelving had previously lived.

When the sheriff pulled the door closed behind himself, he bellowed out a greeting to the apparently empty place, "Jenn, where you at?"

She popped out of the doorway behind the counter with a smile on her face, "Uncle Michael! How are you? Let me get your tea steeping."

Lucy was shocked to find herself looking right at Grasshopper.

Before she had time to school her face, Jenn's eyes shifted to the rest of them and caught on Lucy.

"I'll get tea going for all of you," Jenn said smoothly before turning on an electric kettle and grabbing a bag of loose dried leaves, flowers, and spices. "This is the most popular blend in the area. All the locals love it so much, they can't help but come back for more day after day. My uncle here usually stops by twice a day." Her grin looked sinister. Suddenly, Lucy didn't want any tea. She didn't want Logan or Collin or Betty to have any either. She really didn't give a hoot about the sheriff since he was already on board with whatever Jenn was doing.

"No thank you. I'll just grab a seltzer out of the case over there," Lucy bobbed her head toward the refrigerator case full of juice, soda, and water. "I'll grab a soda or something for you and Collin, too," she said to Logan.

LOGAN

He saw the look on Lucy's face when Jenn stepped up behind the counter. He couldn't say with certainty that she was Grasshopper, but he didn't need to. Lucy's face said it all. This was bad.

Logan heard Lucy's message loud and clear when she offered to get him a soda. She did not want any of them drinking anything made by Jenn.

"I'd love a ginger ale," he responded, "and Collin can't turn down a Barq's root beer." Logan could see it through the glass door of the case. He made eye contact with Collin and was thankful they were still good enough friends to be able to read each other's thoughts in their eyes.

Collin just nodded his agreement and thanked Lucy.

Jenn looked perturbed.

When Logan glanced over at Betty, she was looking around at each of them. It was obvious she knew something was going on, but she didn't know what.

"Fine, just tea for two, then," Jenn snipped.

"Actually, I'm thinking some orange juice would do me some good today. My sugar may be a bit off," Betty may not have understood, but she was siding with them instead of the sheriff and Jenn. Sheriff Clark seemed oblivious to the entire subtext and looked disappointed that none of them were as excited about his niece's tea as he was.

"More for me, I suppose," he said to his niece in a clear effort to soothe her.

In return, Jenn wiped the irritated look from her face and pasted on fake cheer.

"Hey, Jenn, in addition to wanting a cup of tea, we're also wondering if Frank and Jacob are around. Lucy here may have had a bit of a run in with them and one of their floozies."

The flash of offense on Jenn's face made it clear that she knew exactly who he was referring to and did not appreciate being labeled a floozy. But the look passed quickly, "No, I haven't seen them yet today."

"Hm, alright. Will you send me a message later if they swing by? I'd like for Lucy to get a look at them but would prefer not to go hunt them down in the woods. Those boys don't have the good sense God gave a goat," the sheriff was shaking his head as Jenn handed him a mug of tea with the steeper in it.

"Of course, Uncle. Be sure to let that steep for a few minutes, so you'll get the best flavor."

This all felt off, but he wasn't sure how or why. Logan wanted to get Lucy back to their hotel room so she could explain to him what she was thinking.

"You have our statement, Sheriff. We'll be at the Best Western for the next few days. Just give us a call if you need anything else from us." Logan turned to Betty next, "Would you mind giving us a ride?"

"Of course not. Jenn, what do we owe you for the drinks?" Logan had been too distracted by everything else to even think about paying. He was glad to see Collin perk up. No way should Betty be paying for them. She'd already done so much.

Jenn's fake smile became more real when Collin stepped toward the register and held out a twenty-dollar bill.

"I know how nosy Mrs. Sanderson is, and obviously Uncle Michael brought in the other two, but how do you fit into all of this?" Jenn asked with a flirtatious wiggle as she opened the drawer.

"Oh, I'm a friend of Betty's. I'm just stopping by on my way through town."

"Well, you should come back and see me later. I finish up here at eight and can show you all the interesting parts of the area that I'm sure Betty will miss."

"I appreciate the offer," Collin took his change and gave the rest of them a "let's go!" look as he turned and headed for the door.

"You let me know before you leave the area," Sheriff Clark called out to them as he removed the steeper from his tea.

"Will do, Sheriff," Logan replied as he held the door open for everyone else to exit.

They all piled back into Betty's car with Collin up front again. She started the engine but didn't even wait until she was out of the parking lot before addressing them, "Ok, someone explain to me what just happened in there and why I'm drinking sour orange juice instead of whatever magical tea everyone's been going on about for the last few weeks."

Lucy spoke up the second Betty finished, "That was Grasshopper. Jenn is Grasshopper! She recognized me. And why is everyone in town suddenly all about tea? Has this area always been a hot tea kind of place? Logan, did you see the bag of loose tea? It had lots of purple in it. The same color purple as those flowers out in the woods." Her words tumbled out faster than Logan could process.

"Whoa, slow down." He took her hand in his and tried to get her to breathe for a minute. "Let's start with Jenn, who is Grasshopper. That means you met her on the trail. Are you one hundred percent sure it was her?" He didn't want Lucy to think he doubted her, but he also needed to know how confident she was about this.

Luckily, she seemed to understand and took a moment to think before answering, "Yes, I am completely certain that was her. When I set up camp at the shelter, she and the guy, Jacob, I guess, came up a little bit after me. I had to help them set up, and we chatted. It was her face and her voice. Her hair was in a ponytail instead of hanging loose, but it was the same length and color. It was her." Lucy looked Logan square in the eye, and he knew her identification was certain.

"Ok, so Grasshopper is Jenn. If Frank and Jacob often hang out at the store with her, it makes sense that the three of them are working together. The sheriff himself seemed confident that Jacob is Tag-a-long. What were you saying about the tea and flowers, though?"

Lucy started vibrating with energy, so Logan kissed her to slow her down a bit. He rubbed her arms, brushed their noses, and rested his forehead against hers. "Tell us about it slowly enough that we can follow along." He gave her a smirk that he hoped made it clear how much he loved her energy, enthusiasm, and intelligence.

She smiled back before pulling away to explain.

"We saw unusual purple flowers alongside the trail in the area where I found the guns. They were the same color purple as some of the dried tea in the bag that Jenn had. Most hot tea is made from a combination of leaves, flowers, and spices. What if she's using those flowers in her tea?"

This time, Logan was able to follow along with her thoughts. "The sheriff did comment about how the tea was all grown locally. That would make sense for those flowers to be in it, but why would it matter? If it's all about the flowers, why would they have guns out there? Would anyone really try to steal the flowers? They don't even really belong to Jenn. She just finds and harvests them from the woods. I feel like I'm still missing something."

They all sat in silence and thought for a moment.

As they made the final turn toward their hotel, Collin spoke for the first time since they'd gotten in the car, "What kind of purple flowers would be used in tea?"

No one answered him.

Finally, Betty responded as she pulled into a parking spot, "There aren't that many purple flowers around here. At least not ones with big flat petals like you described. We have lots of wildflowers with tiny purple blossoms, and some of them grow in bunches to form purple explosions of flowers, but the petals are tiny. I can't think of too many that are a dark purple either, though I'm certainly not a flower expert. If you had a sample of the plant, I could call up a master gardener friend who specialized in wildflowers. I don't know that we have enough to go on, right now, though."

Collin turned around in his seat to look at Logan, "If I gave you my tablet, do you think the two of you could find a picture of the flower?"

Logan looked at Lucy, "It's worth a shot." She didn't seem confident it would work, but she was willing to try.

"I can also check to see if my picture was uploaded to the cloud before my phone was destroyed."

"I'm supposed to meet some ladies for lunch in a bit. How about we all meet up again around four? I can bring dinner if you don't mind takeout. We have a good Chinese place here."

Logan watched Collin dig out his wallet, so he answered for them, "That sounds perfect. We'll do some research and see you later."

Collin handed Betty money, "You have to let us pay though. You're consulting as a local guide, so we should cover your expenses at the very least."

Betty shook her head but agreed, "Fine, but only because I like you."

They all chuckled and climbed out before Betty drove away.

Logan hated to think of what all she would tell her friends over lunch. He wasn't worried about her saying too much. She'd already proven she could be discreet, when necessary, but he also didn't doubt that she would share a grand adventure tale with them, even if only half of it was true.

Logan used his keycard to open the side door of the hotel for them. Collin paused after he came through the doorway, "Let me run upstairs and grab my tablet for you. While you two research, I need to give my boss a call and file the paperwork to get this started as an official investigation. I'm still not sure what's going on, but knowing the sheriff is related to one of the people involved is enough for me to start things moving."

"Sounds good." Lucy and Logan headed to their room. They set their unopened drinks on the desk and pulled back the curtains to let in the sunshine. Logan was adjusting the thermostat when Collin knocked on the door to drop off his tablet.

Logan climbed up on the bed and sat with his back leaning against the headboard. He patted beside him to encourage Lucy to join him. She brought the tablet. Collin had stuck a post it to the screen with his access code to unlock it. While he started pulling up searches, he noticed Lucy twinge a bit and rub the brace on her wrist.

"Why don't you grab our drinks and some painkillers? It's going to take me a minute to get the search started."

"Yeah, ok. Do you know where the Ibuprofen is?" she asked. "Wait, never mind. Stupid question." It had been on the desk right beside their drinks.

Logan couldn't help but smile and take note of how cute she was and how much he loved her. This whole mess was worth it if it meant he got to spend the rest of his life with her. The realization settled over him with surprising calm. He wanted to spend his life alongside Lucy. He wanted to adventure with her and take care of her and let her lead them through the woods and listen to her laugh and wake up with her beside him every day. The thought should have terrified him, but instead it felt like coming home.

"These got warm. I'm going to grab a bucket of ice for us. I'll leave the door propped." Logan nodded that he understood before she walked out the door leaving the deadbolt out to prevent it from locking behind her.

He pulled up a search window and started typing, already missing her presence in the room.

Chapter 18

COLLIN

Before calling back to his office, he took a few minutes to think about what he knew and jot down some notes. He'd seen a shadow in the back room at the general store. He hadn't thought much of it, but as they'd driven back, he started to second-guess himself. He'd only seen it move once. Could someone have been listening to them the whole time? If it had been Frank or Jacob, what exactly would they have heard?

Collin replayed the conversation in his mind several times before he decided that his gut instinct was right. Anyone in the back room would have heard enough to potentially be dangerous. It had been obvious that Lucy and Jenn recognized each other, and Logan had mentioned where they were staying.

If Collin were one of the bad guys, he'd be unhappy that Lucy was alive and well enough to cause trouble.

They hadn't given away who he was. Even the sheriff didn't know he worked for the FBI, though the man's failure to notice Collin's side arm spoke volumes about his powers of observation and attention to his work. He didn't seem bad for a rural sheriff, but the nature of the job built in conflict. He held an elected position for which he didn't need to earn the competency or training.

The more Collin thought, the more he decided that it would be best to keep a close eye on Logan and Lucy. He didn't see any reason for anyone to try to hurt Logan, but Lucy knew a lot about whatever they were doing, even if she hadn't put the pieces together yet. Between her broken wrist and small stature, she'd be a relatively easy target.

Collin grabbed his phone and laptop and decided to go downstairs to work in their room. He hesitated in their hallway when he realized he might need to call or message them to insure he didn't interrupt anything, but then he looked up and saw their door was propped open. He rolled his eyes and vowed to give them his best lecture about not being stupid prey, but when he knocked and pushed open the door, he only saw Logan sitting on the bed and scrolling through the tablet.

"Hey, man. What's wrong?" Apparently, Logan saw the worry on Collin's face.

"Where's Lucy?" Every tiny molecule inside Collin was screaming at him that bad things were happening.

Logan hopped off the bed as he answered, "She just went out to grab ice. That's why she left the door propped. She should be right back."

They stepped out into the hall to look in the direction of the ice machine. It was around a small corner, so they couldn't see anything.

"Grab your phone and your key card, then lock the door. I'm going to check around the corner and will be right back." Collin hadn't even thought about it before shifting to his professional voice and pulling his weapon from its holster.

Logan didn't argue. He moved to follow Collin's directions while letting Collin make his way down the hall.

When he stepped around the corner, the first thing Collin saw was a scatter of ice cubes across the floor. He followed them back to a bucket left lying on its side on the carpet. There was no sign of Lucy.

He looked further down that hallway and cursed when he saw the outside door at the end. This hotel was shaped like a "V" with the lobby, elevators, and ice machine where the two hallways connected. There was a wall separating the lobby from the hallways, so the ice machine couldn't be seen from the front desk. Both halls ended with a door to the outside that made it easier and more convenient to get to your room from the parking area, exactly like they had done when Betty dropped them off at the end of the other hallway.

There was a chance that Lucy had been pulled into a room along the way or dragged upstairs, but Collin's gut knew that wasn't where she was. He knew she'd been taken out the door, stuffed into a vehicle, and driven away. Lucy was gone.

He heard Logan walking up behind him and tried to figure out what he was going to tell his best friend. When he turned and realized he didn't have to say anything at all, Logan could read it on his face, he couldn't decide if he was relieved or devastated.

Logan just stared at him for a moment.

It was exactly the pause that Collin needed to shift back into his professional persona and do what needed to be done. He put his gun away, took a deep breath, and pulled out his phone.

His boss was immediately supportive. This wasn't exactly the kind of situation the FBI stepped in to help with, but between the local sheriff possibly being involved and the missing person, they could justify getting involved. Collin may have left out his friendship with Logan and just claimed to be visiting a friend in the area when he "discovered" this investigation, but it would be fine. Help was on the way, and he'd allow one of them to take the lead. He wanted to be free to help Logan find Lucy by any means necessary.

"We are going to find her," he told Logan. "We need to start by getting whatever security camera footage they have and review it. If we can get a license plate, we're golden. If we can get a face, we've got it. If we can even get a glimpse of an outfit or vehicle, we've got something to go on."

"I love her. You get that, right? Like, I was just sitting in our room thinking about how I want to marry her." Logan looked at Collin with desperation. He needed reassurance.

"Congratulations. I'll help you pick out the ring. We just need to go reclaim your bride first. Let's go talk to the front desk." He put a hand on Logan's shoulder and started steering him around the wall, out of the hall, and toward the lobby.

The clerk at the front desk was polite but unhelpful. She couldn't have been older than nineteen, and Collin was confident that she was high as a kite. When he asked her about security cameras, her eyes glazed over, she twirled her finger through her hair, and it took more than sixty seconds for her to refocus on him before asking him to repeat the question. She didn't smell like smoke. He was betting heroin or some similar opioid addiction. The glaze over her eyes was a strong indicator. Dealing with that would have to wait. Right now, he needed information to help him find Lucy.

"Security cameras. Where's the footage stored?"

Collin had never seen Logan as happy as he was with Lucy. He was afraid to see how devastated he would be if they found Lucy too late; or worse yet if they never found her at all.

The desk clerk's eyes widened, and she hitched her thumb toward the office space behind the desk. Collin nudged Logan to get them both moving around the desk.

Once in the back, Collin was disappointed to find three old VCRs and three small stacks of VHS tapes. Each stack of tapes was numbered one through ten with either an "A," "B," or "C" after the number. Tapes four A, four B, and four C were all missing, so he guessed they were the ones in the VCRs. The tab that could be removed to stop anyone from recording over footage was still intact on every tape. Collin had seen a few setups like this early in his career. They'd been terrible to work with ten years ago. He knew this would be even worse.

In the nineteen nineties, these kinds of security systems were common. Businesses could set up video cameras that fed to VCRs. The footage was recorded on VHS tapes, saved for a while, and then filmed over when the tapes were reused. Over time, the tapes became worn out and the quality of the footage went from rough to almost indiscernible. Collin couldn't remember the last time he saw VCRs or VHS tapes for sale anywhere, so he figured these tapes were likely old enough to have gone beyond even that. He was worried he might be lucky to see anything more than fuzzy analog snow on the screen.

This also meant that he'd need to take at least one VCR with him to be able to watch the videos, and he'd need to find a TV that still offered the RCA connections used by VCRs. Collin flopped his head back and groaned. This was going to be time consuming, miserable, and was unlikely to yield useful information of any kind. It was the trifecta he dreaded most.

Collin looked over at Logan. Maybe this would be a good task to keep his buddy occupied while Collin explored other avenues of investigation.

"Do you know how to use stuff like this?" He and Logan were the same age, but Collin had only learned about this analog video through his job. He vaguely remembered having a VCR as a kid, but everyone had switched over to DVDs before he was old enough to form solid memories of turning on movies for himself.

Logan looked thoughtful for a minute before replying, "My grandmother had a VCR. I was well into high school before I convinced her to swap it out for a DVD player, so yeah, I know how to use it. But most TVs won't connect to them anymore."

"I know. I'm hoping you could stick around here and try to figure this out, while I check through the neighborhood to see if I can get any better footage from outside cameras belonging to other places."

Logan raised his eyebrows in disbelief, "What other places?"

Collin had to admit that there wasn't much else in the area, but there was a gas station not too far away. That might have something. The benefit to there being little else around was that anyone caught turning from the gas station toward the hotel didn't have anywhere to go except the hotel.

Logan nodded in agreement once Collin explained and agreed to deal with the ancient technology.

LOGAN

There was no way he was going to waste his time looking for old crap that may or may not work. He bullied the desk clerk into giving him the manager's phone number and called to ask the guy how he watched the security footage. Luckily, the manager kept an old TV with built in VCR in his private office for exactly this purpose. When he heard that Logan was working with an FBI agent, he agreed to come in to let Logan into his office and help him find what he needed.

It did take the guy a while to get there, but once he did, he had nothing but good news for Logan. Each VCR recorded from a camera positioned to capture people passing through one of the three main doors of the building. This meant that when

Logan explained Lucy had likely been taken from the hallway where the ice machine was located, the manager immediately knew they should focus on the "B" tapes. Given the short time that she'd been gone before he and Collin had realized she was missing, they figured the four B tape that was currently recording was their best chance. Even better, when Logan expressed concern about the quality of the tape, the manager confessed to hoarding a closet full of new tapes, so that he could swap them out regularly. The current tapes had just been put into rotation a few days earlier.

The footage was still scratchy analog video with wavy lines running through it, but it was clear enough to see an unconscious Lucy being carried out the door. Based on the guy's build, Logan was betting Jacob was the one carrying her. He was far from chunky but wasn't nearly as wafer thin as Frank. Logan was disappointed that the video hadn't captured the vehicle she'd been taken to. Hopefully, Collin had found that on the gas station footage.

Just as Logan was debating spending time looking through the "A" footage from the lobby door, his phone beeped with a message from Collin. He'd struck out at the gas station. They didn't have any cameras that captured traffic making the turn. Collin wanted to meet back up in Logan and Lucy's room to discuss what they knew and what their next steps needed to be. Logan wanted Collin to see the video of Lucy for himself, but the manager was hesitant to leave his office unlocked. Thinking about the front desk clerk, Logan couldn't really fault him for that. He did convince the guy to let him take the entire TV setup back to his room.

"Thank goodness you're here. This stupid TV is awkward as fuck! Can you grab my keycard out of my back pocket and open the door for me?" Logan had not expected the TV to be so challenging to carry. It wasn't that big or heavy, but it was weighted funny. He constantly felt like he was about to drop it. Seeing Collin waiting for him by his hotel room door was a huge relief.

"As much as I would love to grab your ass, how about I take the TV, and you open the door?" Collin started to wrap his own arms around the monstrosity. Logan was happy to release it to him.

Once inside and viewing the tape, Collin agreed that it wasn't much to go on. His coworkers would be arriving in a few hours, but Logan didn't want to wait that long.

"We should call Betty. She might know something."

"I guess she'd be done with her lunch friends by now." Seeing as how it had been more than three hours since they'd parted ways, that seemed reasonable.

Collin dug out his phone to call her. Betty had programmed his number into her phone and answered as soon as it started to ring, "Collin? What's going on?"

Collin had put the phone on speaker so Logan could hear her loud and clear. He could also hear a busy restaurant behind her.

Logan realized that Collin was nodding at him to start the conversation, "Hey, Betty. Sorry to interrupt your lunch. We figured you'd be done by now. We just wanted to get your thoughts. Somebody grabbed, well snatched, I mean, Lucy..." He couldn't bring himself to say it. His whole throat started to close up, and it felt like the room was shrinking around him.

"Breathe, man," he heard Collin say. "Betty, Lucy's been taken. We have footage of her being carried out of the hotel unconscious. We think it's Jacob carrying her, but we aren't certain. Do you know of anywhere they might have taken her?"

There was some shuffling heard on the other end of the line. The background noise faded as it sounded like someone covered the phone. When Betty came back on, she just said, "We'll be at the hotel in fifteen minutes. Be waiting out front."

Sure enough, fifteen minutes later, Betty's Subaru pulled up with a bright purple Honda Fit right behind her. Betty rolled down her window and said, "Hop in. Geri, Linda, and Joan will follow us in Geri's car."

Once everyone was buckled, Betty pulled out of the parking lot with a toss of loose rocks back toward Geri's car.

"Where are we going?" Logan had to ask. Collin had become engrossed in his phone before the car had even been put into drive.

"My FBI team is looking for property owned by Frank, Jacob, or Jenn. Do you know their last names, Betty?"

"Oh, that won't be necessary. Those lazy delinquents don't own much of anything, and Jenn isn't dumb enough to let them use anything in her name. As soon as the girls heard Lucy was missing, they started a list of possible places to find Lucy. We ended up with thirteen places to check out. Four of them are all right together so we're going to start there and knock them off the list quick. Then we'll check the place we think we're most likely to find her."

"Can I see your list and a map? I do have some experience in this area," Collin sounded put out by having his job done by a bunch of old country ladies.

He was sitting up front with Betty, so she had no problem turning to Collin with a glare and asking, "Do you want to find her or not? Those two idiots have been making dumb decisions their entire lives. Joan is their grandmother. She has lots of first-hand experience with their illogical thinking."

Logan sat back when he saw Collin deflate and agree with Betty.

"I do insist that I go in first and that we get some backup. We don't know what we're walking into." Collin made a reasonable point, but Logan just wanted to rush in and find Lucy.

Betty's smile turned mischievous when she replied, "Oh don't worry. We have that covered, too."

The car tires squealed as Betty turned a sharp corner without touching the brakes.

Logan could hear Collin murmuring under his breath as he slammed his fingers into the screen of his phone. Eventually, he appeared to give up on texting and put the phone to his ear.

"I need them here now! Our local contacts think they know where she is and aren't willing to wait for backup."

Collin listened for a moment, but Logan couldn't hear the other side of the conversation.

"No, I'm not willing to call the local police. The sheriff is related to one of our three primary suspects. Tell them to drive faster."

Then Collin held a hand over his phone and turned to Betty, "I at least need addresses for where we're going."

"Put it on speaker."

Collin moved his hand away and returned to the phone conversation, "I'm putting you on speaker. This is our local contact, Betty Sanderson. She's a retired teacher who knows the area and community well. She has several ideas for where the woman may have been taken." Then he clicked one more button on the phone and held it out between himself and Betty. "You're on speakerphone now."

Logan heard the deep rumbly voice on the other end of the line say, "Hello, Mrs. Sanderson. This is Special Agent in Charge Donald Franklin. We certainly appreciate your help, but you really need to wait for more of us to arrive. We should be there in about an hour. Why don't you pull over, maybe get a coffee, and write down that list of addresses? We can move on them as soon as we get there. It would be even more helpful if you could give us the addresses now, so we can do some research on them and prepare ourselves."

Betty scoffed, "S.A.C. Franklin, where are you based out of?"

"I'm sending people from Albany. It won't take them long. Please be patient."

"Where are you from, sir?" Betty was more insistent this time.

"I'm in Virginia, ma'am."

"Yeah, that's what I figured. Have you personally spoken to the agents you're sending?"

"I'm in contact with their supervisor."

"Agent Warner," Franklin's voice sharpened considerably, "I need you to take control of this situation immediately. Mrs. Sanderson, with all due respect, this is now a federal investigation. I'm ordering you to stand down and wait for backup. Agent Warner, you are to secure the civilians and maintain your position until additional agents arrive. Do I make myself clear?"

Collin shifted uncomfortably but before he could respond, Betty jumped back in.

"Not what I asked but let me just get to the point." There was a pause as Betty slowed the car and started to turn onto a gravel road. She pulled over and let the Fit go by before pulling out behind it. "SAC Franklin, I understand you have protocols, and I respect that. But here's what you don't understand. There are no addresses. We're going to unmarked, secret places tucked into the national forest. It will be another fifteen minutes at least before we arrive at our first destination. These places are not on your maps. Google has not taken street views of them. Law enforcement gets shot at upon arrival, and some of these idiots have trail cams up to ensure they see you before you see them."

"Mrs. Sanderson, I don't care if—"

"Let me finish, sir. Your people from Albany? They don't know this terrain. They'll spend an hour just finding the turn-off roads, assuming they can navigate the unmarked forest service routes at all. Agent Warner can drop a pin when we find her so your people can locate us, but right now, time is critical. You're not equipped to deal with this specific situation, and every minute we wait gives them more opportunity to move her or destroy evidence."

"Agent Warner, I'm giving you a direct order to—"

"SAC Franklin," Betty's voice took on the tone of a principal dealing with a difficult school board member, "Agent Warner can follow your orders if you want to explain to his supervisors why a kidnapped woman died while federal agents sat in a hotel parking lot waiting for backup that doesn't know the area. Or he can come with locals who've been dealing with these particular criminals for decades and actually have a chance of bringing her home alive."

The line was quiet for several long seconds before Franklin's voice came back, tight with controlled anger. "Agent Warner, you understand that if this goes sideways, it's on both of you. I want constant updates, and at the first sign of trouble, you call for immediate extraction. This is against my better judgment and every protocol we have."

"Understood, sir," Collin replied quietly.

"And Mrs. Sanderson, if any of my people get hurt because of this civilian operation..."

"They won't," Betty said firmly. "We'll call you once we've found her. Have your people ready to process a crime scene." Betty became surprisingly chipper as she ended the conversation and nodded at Collin, "You should hang that up now."

Collin looked a bit shocked but did as she said.

"Betty, we can't do this. I can't take my best friend and four little old ladies into this kind of danger."

"You're exactly right. That's why you aren't taking us anywhere. We are being kind enough to take you with us as we rescue his girlfriend." She vaguely tipped her head back toward Logan when she said "his." The gravel road was too rough, and they were going too fast for her to risk pulling a hand away from the wheel.

Collin seemed to think for a moment before resigning himself to the situation.

Logan wanted to jump in, but he was legitimately unsure which side he was on. It sounded like Betty and her friends were their best shot at getting Lucy back, but he was not comfortable putting them at risk. And this was starting to sound like a bigger risk than he could have ever imagined.

Then again, maybe it was another piece of the puzzle. As Logan forced his brain to shift away from thoughts of Lucy, he realized that he'd barely started his research into the purple flowers, but he had found the picture he'd taken. By some miracle, it had been uploaded before his phone was destroyed.

"Collin, let me see your tablet again."

"Sure, but why?" Collin asked as he handed it back.

It only took Logan a moment to unlock it. The picture was still pulled up on the screen. He leaned forward and showed it to Collin, "This is the picture I took of the flowers we found. Any idea what they are?"

Collin squinted at it for a minute but looked uncertain.

Betty glanced over but couldn't take the time to really look. She did comment, "Geri will know. She's a master naturalist who specialized in flowers. I think I mentioned her before."

Collin's investigative mind seemed to turn back on, "What kind of places are we going to, Betty? I don't mean like addresses, but are they stills or storage or what?"

Betty smiled, "Now you're asking smart questions. There are three stills down low on our list. There wouldn't be much place for Lucy there, so they're unlikely. Our first stop is an old homestead that has part of a barn, part of a shed, and the foundation of a house left standing. There's also a newer one room cabin in the area. By "newer" I mean that Joan's grandfather built it for hunting. It's still old and decrepit, but last time we saw it, there was still a roof and a door. Frank and Jacob know about it, but Joan isn't sure they've ever been there. That's why we don't expect to find Lucy there, but it's the biggest place on the list and closest to the road, so crossing it off first made sense to us."

Collin and Logan both grabbed onto the frame of the car as they bounced through a missing chunk of the road. Logan wasn't willing to call something bigger than the vehicle a "pothole." At one point, he was pretty sure all four wheels were in the hole before they bounced back out.

"The next stop is a brand-new cabin. Frank and Jacob were hired to help build it for some seasonal guy who wanted it to be his rugged vacation home. He lost all his money in twenty eighteen, so he never finished paying anyone. I don't know if he still owns the property or not, but it's the one Frank and Jacob would be most familiar with. It was supposed to be designed to be accessible by four-wheeler in the summer and snow mobile in the winter, and it's entirely off the grid. They had to clear a road big enough to bring in materials when they started to build it, so we're thinking that might still be passable enough to let us get back there. If not, we'll have to hike out."

Collin looked back at Logan with a look of disbelief on his face.

Logan just shrugged. He was willing to do whatever he needed to get Lucy back.

"Ok," Collin sighed. "Logan, do you still go to the range?"

"Every once in a while, but not that often. I can handle a gun, though."

Collin pulled his spare out of his ankle holster and started to hand it to him, but Betty stopped him.

"Put that back." She couldn't say much. The "road" was washboard, narrow, and muddy. "Just hang on."

Within seconds, they saw brake lights come on in the Honda and both vehicles stopped right there in the road. There was nowhere to pull off or park. Apparently, they were just going to park right there.

Logan looked around and decided it wasn't likely to be the dumbest or most dangerous thing they did that day. They hadn't seen a single other car since turning onto the gravel road.

"Everybody out," Betty announced cheerfully as she turned off the engine.

All four older ladies congregated around the back of Geri's car and one of them waved Collin and Logan over to join them.

The woman Logan assumed was Geri opened the back hatch and lifted the floor of the trunk to reveal the spare tire well. She must have been confident in her tires' performance, because there was no spare. Instead, the space had been modified to hold a shotgun, two rifles, and four nine mm handguns. There were also several boxes of assorted ammunition. Logan turned to Collin just in time to see his friend's face light up with glee. Collin might not want these women to put themselves at risk, but he was clearly excited to see their arsenal.

As Geri and Betty started sorting through the goods, the other two women turned to Collin and Logan to introduce themselves.

"I'm Linda." The chubbiest of the four had her hair permed into the pale, wispy helmet of hair that was so common for older grandmothers. Her handshake was firm, but Logan was betting she was well over seventy years old.

"I'm sorry we couldn't meet under better circumstances," said the other woman. "I'm Joan." She stuck out her hand as well but didn't appear nearly as confident. She had her brown hair cut to a chin length bob. It was thinning, and the brown looked more like a dye job than natural coloring, but her face had limited wrinkles. "I am so sorry my grandsons are putting you through this. You're Logan, right?"

"Yes, ma'am. Any idea what they're doing out here that they wouldn't want Lucy to know about?"

Joan dropped her hand from his and looked at him for a minute before answered, "I hate to admit this, but they got most of their smarts from their father, which means they didn't get much. Their mother and I tried to push them in school and make them understand how important it was for them to learn a trade or something, but..." she trailed off.

"Most children don't do what their parents want or expect," Logan tried to chime in helpfully.

"Oh, I'm afraid they did exactly what their good for nothing father wanted. I will never understand what my daughter saw in him. She didn't divorce him until he'd been in prison for more than five years. Even after he was sentenced to life, she tried to "stay committed" to him. I can't help but think things might have been different had he gone away when the boys were younger. Frank was sixteen before his dad got busted." Joan shook her head, "In any case, I'm sorry that any branch of my family tree got mixed up in hurting you."

Logan certainly appreciated both her sentiment and her help finding Lucy. He told her as much before Geri caught his attention and asked if he preferred a nine mm or a rifle.

Her crazy red curls reminded him a grandmotherly version of Merida from the Disney movie, Brave. Logan wanted to guess that Geri was the youngest of the group, but he wasn't confident enough to place any money on it. He was betting they were all above sixty.

He certainly wanted to be one of the first through the door to find Lucy, so he opted for a nine mm. He'd been honest when he told Collin that he did go shoot occasionally, but he'd never had any interest in killing an animal or a person. He thought shooting paper targets was great sport and plenty of stress relief. Then again, the thought of someone putting their hands on Lucy made him feel very friendly toward the trigger. He could handle taking a life if it meant saving hers.

Logan caught Collin looking at him with a raised eyebrow. His friend knew how he felt about guns. He nodded at Collin to let him know that he could handle whatever they faced.

Each of the women opted for a long barrel gun. Linda said she couldn't aim for shit, so she took the shotgun and filled her pockets with bear shot. It might not kill a man, but it would slow them down enough for one of the others to intervene.

Betty, Geri, and Joan all checked their rifles like they'd done it a million times before. Geri also pulled out a holster to clip on her belt and added a nine mm. Based on the look on Collin's face, he was as surprised by all of this as Logan was.

"Joan knows the property the best, so she'll lead the way. The three of us," Geri waved her hand to indicate herself, Linda, and

Betty, "will hang back to provide backup and support while you all go in."

Logan got the impression there might be more to Geri than met the eye. Collin also seemed to be analyzing her a bit more closely.

From there, Joan took over with explaining the plan, "We're going to circle around the edge of the property. We can enter the clearing right by the newest cabin. That will let us check that out first, since it's the most likely place we'll find them."

"Sounds like the best plan we're going to get," Collin agreed and prepared to follow Joan into the woods.

Chapter 19

Her head hurt again. She was really fucking sick of waking up after being drugged. At least she wasn't left in the middle of the woods this time, though once she tugged on her hands and found them hogtied to her feet, she regretted that thought and started wishing for the woods. Also, her nose itched. Because of course her nose would itch when her hands were tied to her feet leaving her with no way to scratch.

She turned to rub her nose on her shoulder and realized that she did still have clothes on (Yay!) and she was on top of a pile of hay. Admittedly, it might be straw. She didn't know the difference. Lucy rolled her eyes at herself. Straw versus hay was not the primary concern right now. In the process of scratching her nose on the shoulder of her shirt sleeve, she had knocked a chunk of hair across her face. It was now tickling her cheek. This was worse than the nose itch.

Tying a person's hands to their feet should be consider an inhumane form of cruel and unusual punishment. She was so annoyed she couldn't even start thinking about where she might be or what she needed to do or whatever the smart thing would be to think about in this situation. She shook her head back and forth to try and move the hair away from her face. All that did was shake more hair loose.

This was ridiculous. She needed to think. Okay, Lucy, she thought to herself, you can do this. She let her head fall back on the straw-hay behind her and closed her eyes. What did she know? Mentally, she started a list:

She had been drugged.

She had been taken from the hotel while getting ice.

Logan would be quick to notice her missing.

He and Collin would start looking for her right away.

She took a deep breath preparing to scream and holler with the hope that someone could hear her, but then she stopped and reminded herself to take it one step at a time. What else did she know?

She hadn't seen the person who stabbed her with a needle, but she did remember the sensation of it stinging her neck. When she listened closely, she heard sounds of the forest, though there was a roof over her head. She was in a barn or similar out-building.

Oh, she should smell. Growing up in a rural community, she'd visited enough friends' farms to learn that chicken coops smelled different from horse barns. She'd be hopeless if it were pigs or goats or something, but there might be enough there to give her more information. She inhaled through her nose, thought for a moment, and tried it again. There was no animal smell. She mostly smelled hay or straw or whatever and a wet, musty, rotting-wood odor. Considering the lack of animal noises, she was disappointed to decide that made sense.

Still, this was more information. Looking around as best she could, she noticed light filtering between boards and places where chunks of some boards had broken off. So, she was in an abandoned out-building somewhere in the woods. Well, crap. That would not make it easy for Logan and Collin to find her.

Lucy was running out of ideas. She also noticed the light was casting longer shadows. She was betting that it was evening, and darkness would soon descend. Lucy sighed. It was time to self-rescue. Thanks to everything she'd been through the past two years, this thought didn't scare her or even make her nervous. She'd developed a confidence in her ability to take care of herself no matter the situation. It did make her tired, though. Having Logan alongside her had been so comforting. It would have been nice to have someone with her to help with the rescue.

She drummed up her motivation and enthusiasm by reminding herself that she could get back to him once she got herself out of this mess. It was time to go to work. Lucy knew that getting free of the ropes was her first task. Once that was done, freedom was hers for the taking... well, unless there were people with guns hanging around outside, but she could figure that out once she could move around.

Lucy flexed her hands and feet as hard as she could before relaxing them. With her hands tied to her feet, she couldn't get her mouth close enough to tug at the knots with her teeth. Luckily, the rope they had tied her with was slippery enough to loosen as she flexed and relaxed. Clearly, her kidnappers were not Boy Scouts. Once it loosened enough for her to start rotating her wrists and wiggling her feet, she was able to slide one hand free. After that it was easy. She made a mental note to hogtie people behind their backs instead of in front of them if she ever needed to restrain someone like this.

Once free and able to look around more, she discovered she was in the back corner of an old storage barn. There was a work bench across from her along with lots of old, rusty tools, and a three-wheeled tractor with a missing front tire sat in the center of the space. Lucy crept along the edge of the barn and stepped slowly and gently to limit the squeaking and creaking of old boards as much as possible.

She listened for a few minutes before starting her search through the tools on the work bench. The wind was picking up, but she didn't hear any humans sounds. When the boards did groan and complain, she hoped anyone within earshot would attribute it to the wind blowing through.

Most of the old tools could be useful, but there wasn't any particular one that jumped up and screamed, "I'm a weapon that you can defend yourself with!" There was a hammer she could use to bludgeon someone, or a giant wrench that could be used similarly. When she picked up the wrench, though, she rethought that idea. By the time she convinced her muscles to get it up high enough to do any damage, Frank or whomever would be halfway to Russia.

The bench had a few old metal files lying around. They looked stabby enough to be useful, but Lucy wasn't sure the flattish end of them was what she needed. When she saw the handle of a screwdriver, she knew she'd hit the jackpot. An image of herself dressed like Buffy the Vampire Slayer with a hammer in one hand a screwdriver in the other flashed through her mind. She envisioned herself as a badass fighter with a tool in each hand using the hammer to drive the screwdriver into Frank's chest with a vengeance.

Then she remembered she was Lucy and not Buffy and tried to add some reality to her vision. Suddenly, she pictured Frank laughing at her when she missed with the screwdriver and was forced to wail at his chest with the hammer leaving nothing but deep round bruises. Ugh! What else was here?

"You are such a dumbass, Jacob!"

Oh, shit! That was Frank's voice. There was no time left to search. Lucy grabbed for the hammer and screwdriver but accidentally knocked the hammer to the floor.

"What was that?"

The wind couldn't mask the sound of a hammer hitting the floor. Frank and Jacob were heading this way. Lucy kept hold of the screwdriver as she darted back over to the corner where she had been tied up. She tried to curl up similarly to how she'd been before while carefully angling her feet and hands away from the door where the men would enter.

"I'm telling you, Frank, I hog-tied her with her hands and feet together. There's no way she could get free."

"But you didn't check her for weapons, did you?"

"She doesn't have anything, and even if she did, it wouldn't do her any good all tied up."

Frank and Jacob were in the barn.

"You dumbass!! You left her in a barn full of tools and shit, too? You better be damn glad she didn't get free."

Lucy was now certain she was going to die. Frank was already angry, and he was about to find her freed from her bonds with a screwdriver clasped in her hand. She didn't have any fighting skills, but she knew that driving a screwdriver into a person's body wasn't nearly as easy as it looked in movies and on TV. She'd need to aim for groin, neck, or face. But there was no way she could fight off both Frank and Jacob. If she had a blade, she might have been able to slice an ankle or knee to immobilize them.

As a teen, Lucy had been foolishly brave. When friends asked her how or why she did things, her answer was the same, "The worst that could happen was that I would die, and I was okay with that, so I gave it my best shot."

This was a situation for teenaged Lucy. She was probably going to die, but she'd try her best to fight her way free. As she listened to the men get closer, she let her mind spend a moment appreciating the best parts of her life. It allowed her breathing to slow down and gave her a sense of calm.

LOGAN

There had been nothing but a family of raccoons on the property. That poor family had one less parent thanks to Collin, though Logan couldn't blame him after the way the animal had come screaming and screeching down from one of the high beams in the second building they'd checked.

They'd started with the cabin. Logan's heart had been racing despite the lack of any sound or scuffed ground that would suggest a human presence. Checking through windows had not uncovered any signs of life, so no one had been surprised to find nothing but dust and cobwebs once they got inside.

The second building had relieved Logan's disappointment at not finding anything in the cabin. It was an old woodshed with no door on the frame, but the windowless walls and roof were still intact. The floor was hardpacked dirt, but the entryway looked freshly disturbed. Logan didn't see any footprints, but it was clear someone or something had passed through the doorway since the last rain.

Collin held him back and entered first. The silence brought up images in Logan's mind of a still and lifeless Lucy that Logan had to forcefully shove away so that he could focus on what was happening in front of him. Collin ducked around the edge of the door frame, flashing his light in front of him and started to call "All clear" when it happened.

A high-pitched scream rang through the air, immediately followed by a single shot and a thump. Instead of silence, more screaming and screeching ensued, and a very rattled Collin darted back out through the door and shooed them all away from the opening.

Just behind him came an insanely angry raccoon with her head tucked low, fur puffed, back arched, and teeth bared. She hissed and snarled at them while blocking the doorway. Then Collin explained that there were several young racoons behind her. The second adult had been high up in the rafters when Collin entered. The single shot they'd heard had signaled that one's death.

Everyone felt a bit traumatized by the whole thing but had been relieved when the rest of their search had been downright boring. Unfortunately, there was still no sign of Lucy.

Logan's nerves were frayed, and he was struggling to hold himself together as they headed back to the cars. He wanted to laugh about one raccoon parent but cry about the other. He wanted to tease his friend about being bested by an animal and yell at him for not finding Lucy. When he looked down and saw how badly he was shaking, Betty placed her hand gently on his arm and reminded him, "We didn't think she'd be here. Our next stop is a more likely place to find her, but if she's not there, we'll keep checking our way down the list."

He took strength from her confidence, nodded, and taking a deep breath, climbed into her car to head to their next stop.

After suffering through Betty's insane driving in reverse the whole way to the end of the road before she could turn around, Logan was thrilled to see the road to their second destination was passable. While it had become overgrown in the past four or five years, recent tire tracks had already knocked down any saplings that had tried to grow. The ground was rutted, and Logan was sure they'd driven through a bush at one point, but none of it had stopped the Subaru or the Honda. Once they arrived in the clearing where construction on the house had been started, Betty did a tight circle to park the car facing back out the way they'd come from and waited for Geri to park beside her.

"I figure we should be ready for a quick get-away," she said seriously to Collin.

Thinking about how not-stealthy they were being, Logan couldn't resist pointing out "We just bounced and bobbed our way straight up through the woods and parked smack in front of the house!"

Collin gave him side-eye glare. To Betty he simply said, "Thank you. It's always a good idea to park facing out."

They all climbed out of the cars and stood in the driveway looking around. About an acre of land around the cabin had been cleared. It was overgrown in many places and bare dirt in others. In general, the property looked like an old, abandoned construction site. Logan noted that there were several patches of wildflowers growing around the clearing, but none of them looked like the purple ones he and Lucy had seen on the trail. That thought reminded him to ask Geri if she could identify the flowers.

"Hey, where's your tablet? I want to show Geri the picture I got of the flowers," he asked Collin.

"I left it on the front seat."

He was feeling like this stop would also turn up empty, but maybe he could learn more about why Frank and company were so upset about what Lucy had found. Retrieving Collin's tablet, he got Geri's attention and showed her the picture of the flower, while Collin went over to poke his head into the nearby garage.

"Where did you say you took this picture?" she asked.

"Just off the trail between VT9 and the Daniel Webster Monument up by Stratton Mountain. Why?"

"Are you sure? These are poppies that usually grow in central Asia. I've never seen them around here. I didn't know that they could grow anywhere on this continent even."

"They were spread out all over through the trees along that stretch of trail. Lucy and I both saw them."

Collin had returned and was devoting his full attention to their conversation, "Wait, did you say poppies?"

When Geri nodded, he went on, "Do you know what kind of poppies?"

"Not off the top of my head. Like I said, they aren't native to the area. The only reason I'm even sure they're poppies is because of the time I spent in the UK. Red poppies are frequently used as a kind of memorial there."

Collin grabbed the tablet from Logan but immediately looked disappointed, "Not enough signal for internet."

Logan opened his mouth to suggest they move on the next site. This one was clearly empty, and he wanted to find a better signal so Collin could figure out whatever it was he was on the verge of understanding. Before he could make a sound, Collin perked up and held up a hand to stop him. Three of the four older ladies were all tuned in and went silent as well. Everyone held their breath, and then Collin asked quietly, "Did you hear that?"

Geri rolled her eyes and looked at Collin like he was stupid. Linda continued to scan the area apparently oblivious to the rest of them. Betty explained, "Linda lost her hearing aid last week. She can't hear squat. Joan's hearing aid does pretty well but only focuses on nearby sounds. Geri hears okay, but she's no spring chicken, and I used up all my good hearing back in the classroom. So, no, we didn't hear it." Then she turned to ask Logan, "How about you?"

He shook his head. Whatever Collin heard was too faint for his ears.

"Are there any other buildings on the property?" Collin asked as he handed the tablet back to Logan. "There was an old van in the garage. It didn't look like much, but it might still run."

Betty looked at the other three women before shrugging. "I don't think any of us know. The city guy owned this property long before he decided to build on it. None of us know it well. We just know Frank and Jacob had been working out here. Was the van brown? That's what Frank drove and sometimes lived in."

"Yeah, it was." Logan's heart rate sky-rocketed with Collins confirmation, but they still didn't know where Lucy was. He wanted to run and find her but didn't know which way to go.

Then they heard the shriek. Logan wasn't sure if it was human or animal, but it sounded more pissed than distressed. In any case, when Collin looked at Logan, he immediately suggested, "Let's go!"

Chapter 20

LUCY

It was during her final calm moment that Lucy realized what Frank had said. Jacob hadn't checked her for weapons. She wore her neck knife tucked inside her bra, nestled into her cleavage for so long, she never even noticed it anymore. As quietly as she could, she drew one hand up to her chest, and there it was. She had a knife! Sure, it was only about two inches long, but it was easy to hold onto and sharp. She could work with that.

Aiming for the torso would be useless. Her blade was too short to do anything more than annoy someone, and if she hit a rib, it would barely do that. If she could get their neck, she could do considerable damage. Even slicing through an armpit or back of the knee could be crippling.

Think, Lucy, she encouraged herself. She was lying on straw just off the ground, and they would approach her on foot. Surprise was her biggest advantage. She needed to go for the ankles. If she could slice through an Achilles tendon or something similar, she could immobilize them while she got away. It might not solve things if they had a gun, but even then, it might buy her enough time to get the gun away from them.

The bigger problem was that there were two of them. She'd only be able to take one by surprise. Please, let it be Frank, she silently wished upon the universe. Jacob might be much bigger, but he was also dumb enough that Lucy stood a healthy chance at outsmarting him. Frank... well, Frank wasn't smart by any means, but he was sly and cunning and wily. She'd much rather face off against big and dumb.

She heard one set of footsteps approaching her. At least they weren't both coming over together.

"See, she's fine. Still tied up just where I left her." Lucy could hear Jacob's voice farther away, which meant it was Frank coming her way. Fortune was on her side.

Lucy waited and waited and waited. Frank was approaching with caution. Finally, she tried wiggling like she was trying to move with her hands and feet still tied. That brought Frank closer.

She could hear one step and then another. He was almost there. Lucy wanted to be sure he was close enough for her to swing her hand behind him and catch the back of his ankle when she made her move.

One last step, and she could see the top of his head at the edge of her peripheral vision. She pressed the outside of her leg against the ground to roll over onto her back and face him. She did not want her hands trapped below her.

The screwdriver was still in Lucy's left hand, but with her fractured wrist, she couldn't do much with it. Mostly she kept ahold of it in case she lost her knife. She'd chosen a neck knife with a T-shaped handle. This allowed her to brace the base of the handle against the palm of her hand while the slim center of the handle rested between her middle and ring fingers before connecting to the blade.

As soon as she'd rolled, she reached out and slashed with all her might before pulling back and stabbing anything and everything she could get to. She started low but moved higher as she struck repeatedly. She'd managed a few good hits before Frank crashed to the ground, grabbing his leg and swearing. Lucy tossed away the screwdriver to free her hand to help her get up from the ground.

Jacob was looking at the scene like he wasn't sure what was happening. He might have been waiting for Frank's orders. Lucy decided not to give him any opportunity to figure it out. She yelled the loudest shriek she could muster and leapt toward him with her knife in her right hand and her left elbow tucked tightly in beside her waist. She fully intended to drive the knife into Jacob's throat or face with everything she had.

Her sense of righteous satisfaction started with the look of fear on his face and didn't abate until he was lying still in a pool of his own blood. In the background, she was dimly aware of Frank screaming at Jacob to kill her. Once Jacob was still, she turned around to find that Frank had made it to a seated position against the wall and was grabbing whatever he could find within reach and throwing it at her. Mostly it was straw, but he did manage to chuck the screwdriver in her direction.

Before Lucy could even contemplate what to do about Frank, Jenn pulled open the barn door and asked what all the ruckus was about.

"This stupid, crazy woman," Frank sputtered in anger and pain.

Jenn took a step further into the barn before spotting Lucy standing over Jacob's body. She glanced back and forth between Lucy, Jacob's body, and Frank.

"Well, don't just stand there. Come and help me!" Frank screeched at her while squirming around futilely on the ground.

Lucy wasn't sure what to do with him. She couldn't imagine killing him, especially when he was already immobilized, but she loved the idea of knocking him unconscious. She couldn't determine how to make that happen without putting herself at more risk and that didn't seem like the most brilliant idea.

The furious look on Jenn's face made Lucy wonder if maybe Jenn would take care of Frank for her. She could picture Jenn walking over to him and driving her thumbs through his eyeballs or slashing his throat with whatever she could find nearby. Then she looked back at Jacob's body and had to stop herself from blowing chunks. Now was not the time for her to ruminate on what she'd just done.

Lucy shoved those thoughts down and turned back to Jenn. She was still standing between Lucy and the only exit. Frank tried calling her over again. Jenn could help Frank, attack Lucy, or...

A brief moment of thought crossed Jenn's face before her decision became clear.

She turned and ran.

LOGAN

Sound traveled in unusual ways in the mountains. Sometimes the earth would dampen a noise until it almost disappeared. Other times, vibrations would bounce off rocks to amplify, change direction, or both. Logan had been certain the shriek he'd heard came from the ridge behind the house and directly in front them right until Collin started to take off to their left, convinced it had come from that way.

Geri halted them both and started giving orders, "Collin, take Joan and start working your way around the clearing counterclockwise. Look for any kind of trail to follow. Logan, you come with me, and we'll start clockwise. Betty, stay with Linda. We'll holler for back up if we need you. Just try to keep an eye on where we enter the tree line, so you know which way to go based on whose voice calls you.

Everyone agreed, checked their weapons, and started walking. It wasn't long before Logan and Geri spotted a well-traveled trail. "Should we call for the others?" Logan asked Geri.

"Just holler that we found a trail to follow, but don't holler too loud. Betty'll hear us, and I don't want to make it obvious to whoever's up there that we're here."

Logan kept it to a simple, "Found a trail." Then he waved at Betty when she looked over at him. He started to follow Geri through the undergrowth, but she paused and bent over.

When she stood back up, she was holding the sheriff's business card. There was no way to know if it had come from the sheriff himself or someone else. Logan vaguely remembered him handing a card to himself, Lucy, and Collin when he'd interviewed them.

Geri put her finger to her lip in a silent request that Logan stay quiet. As much as he wanted to yell for everyone to come running, he understood that it might be best not to announce their arrival. He kept his mouth shut and trailed behind Geri as she continued to climb up the steep hillside following the narrow trail.

As they got farther from the cabin, he saw remnants of an old plow and some wire fencing. He thought there was an old wheel off in the distance away from the trail, and then he recognized what he thought were parts of an old still beneath a mostly collapsed and rotted roof.

He hadn't been able to see the cabin for a while now, and the climb kept getting steeper. They'd been hiking for less than five minutes, but they'd been moving quickly, and the forest was thick around them. It felt like they would hit the top of the ridge soon when he heard an animal crashing toward them from above.

He grabbed Geri and pulled her off the trail just in case it was a bear that wanted to use the path. Whatever it was sounded big. It must have been plenty loud for Geri to hear as well. She didn't hesitate to move off to the side with him. She pulled out her rifle and rested the barrel on a nearby tree branch so she could take aim and hold it steady without shaking from supporting the gun's weight.

Someday Logan was going to get this woman to tell him her story. What kind of crazy, red-haired, bush woman knew how to balance a rifle on a tree branch in order to give herself the best aim and control?

The sounds were still heading in their direction. Based on how long it was taking the animal to get to them, Logan realized they were farther from the top than he'd expected. It didn't surprise him. Every time he went hiking, he rediscovered how close the top of a ridge could feel and look while remaining far, far away.

Eventually, the animal got close enough for them to hear it huffing and puffing. It was breathing fast. And hard. And making strange noises. Logan listened more closely, "stupid... fucking... fuck... ouch...shit... son of a... oof... eep!" It was a human animal.

Logan moved out from the tree he'd ducked behind as he watched Geri take a deep, calming breath and put her eye to the sight of her gun. Shit! She was going to shoot. What if it was Lucy? Logan grabbed Geri's arm to stop her from pulling the trigger.

She glared at him. Hard and cold. "What do you think you're doing?" she hissed quietly.

"What if it's Lucy?"

"It's not!"

Geri appeared to be completely certain about this. Logan wanted to trust her, but she was old. Also, what if she was involved. Was she trying to shoot Lucy? Maybe she knew exactly what the flowers were and was now trying to cover it up.

Logan shook himself. He was losing it. The woman, and it was a woman, hurtled around the final bend, and Logan was able to see Jenn for himself. Unfortunately, it was too late for either him or Geri to do anything about it. When Jenn saw them, she threw herself directly into them with wailing fists, angry knees, and even a headbutt that had to have done more damage to her skull than it had to Logan's chest.

Still, Logan was struggling to get a solid grip on Jenn. She kept trying to bite him and kick him in his special place. This woman was nuts, but Logan was still reluctant to hit her. That just felt wrong to him. He just wanted to subdue her and determine what was happening.

With no weapon, she wasn't doing much damage, but she also wasn't stopping. Logan was trying to wrestle her down so that he might sit on her, but it felt like that time an old ex-girlfriend had asked him to give her cat oral medication. For the record, he'd broken up with the girl immediately after the fact. Anyone who wanted to own something that tiny but that vicious wasn't right in the head.

Come to think of it, that was a perfect description of Jenn: tiny, vicious, and not right in the head. He might have to slug her after all.

"Incoming!" Geri's shout got his attention, but not in time.

Chapter 21

LUCY

Lucy had considered letting Jenn go on her merry way. It would give her time to pull herself together, but Lucy still didn't know where they were, nor had she determined what to do with Frank. So, really it would just mean Jenn was on the loose and Lucy would be lost in the woods again. So, it made more sense to follow the lunatic to a road or house or someplace where she could properly give the witch what she deserved.

She sighed and headed off down the trail Jenn had just taken. It wasn't well-traveled, but there was enough there for her to follow. She wasn't moving nearly as comfortably as Jenn, so whenever she felt like Jenn was getting too far away, she'd have to run to make up some ground before losing her breath and slowing back to a walk.

All the hiking had done wonders for her stamina. Despite her entire body hurting, she was able to keep Jenn within hearing distance without exhausting herself. Then she heard the fighting. At first, she had hope that Jenn was being attacked by a bear. Unfortunately, life was never that just. The growling and swearing clearly sounded more like Logan than a bear.

Which meant Logan had found her, but also Jenn was attacking Logan. Lucy's brow furrowed with disapproval before she charged down the trail at full speed. As Lucy rounded one last bend in the trail, Logan and Jenn became visible. They were still standing, but Jenn was like a rabid animal going after Logan.

Lucy willed her legs to pump faster while picking her feet up high so she wouldn't trip over roots or rocks. She felt like she was flying through the woods as she hurled her body into Jenn's. There was no plan. She took no aim. Lucy simply threw her entire self into the vile woman and assaulted her with fists and nails and feet and teeth. At one point, Lucy thought she might have even used her forehead to bash in Jenn's nose.

By the time she felt Logan's arms band tightly around her pulling her away, her vision cleared enough to see Jenn lying curled up on the ground, clutching her face in her hands, moaning, and rocking.

"Easy, beautiful, easy. You got her. She's down. It's okay now. You're ok. She can't hurt anyone else now. I'm ok. We're both here."

As Logan's soothing voice finally broke through the red haze in her brain, Lucy curled into his body and realized that she was sobbing, and her throat was raw from screaming and shrieking at Jenn. It took her another minute to finish processing. She focused on the feel of Logan's chest and arms, the sound of his voice, and the scent of his shirt. As her muscles relaxed, she felt his arms wrap more tightly around her. Somehow, he'd lowered them both to sit on the ground. She was facing him, straddling his lap. By the relaxed way he was sitting, she could tell he was leaning against a tree or rock or something.

As her sobbing slowed to sniffles, Logan's voice shifted from gentle murmuring to meaningful words, "Hey, you ok? Back with us?"

"Yeah. I just... she..." images of Frank falling to the ground, Jacob's lifeless body, and Jenn grappling with Logan all flashed through her mind. She didn't even know where to start.

She had killed a man.

Her sniffles started to escalate again, but Logan interrupted her, "It's okay, Lucy. You're safe. It's okay. Your attack on Jenn was impressive. I knew you were fierce, but damn, remind me never to make you angry."

Lucy could hear the smile and pride in Logan's voice. It was exactly what she needed to enable her to take one more deep breath and start explaining.

"I killed Jacob. And Frank's up in the barn with a leg too sliced up to walk on." Lucy looked at her hands. She'd pulled back from Logan enough to splay them across his chest and was absentmindedly rubbing them on his shirt. It was flannel and felt soothing and soft and comforting. But she'd smeared blood and snot and tears all over his shirt, too.

"I don't know where my knife is." She thought she'd pulled it out from… nope… no thinking about what she'd done to Jacob. She was going to need therapy after this adventure.

"Your neck knife?" Logan had been the one to hang the cord around her neck and nestle the knife in her cleavage that morning. Had it really just been that morning?

"It's okay, it's okay. We'll find it or get you a new one." Logan suddenly sounded concerned.

"No, I just…" Lucy sighed, dragged herself out of her own swirling thoughts, and forced herself to talk. "I was thinking that it's been a really long day."

Logan chuckled and nodded his agreement.

"I killed a man."

"To save yourself. Because you are strong and fierce and don't let anything or anyone stand in your way. It's one of the things I love most about you."

"I hate to break up this sweet scene, but we probably ought to do something with this one, and it sounds like there's a couple bodies up the hill that need to be taken care of," interrupted Geri.

Lucy looked up to see an older woman with crazy, curly red hair flying in all directions. She was cradling a rifle and had a handgun clipped to her belt. Lucy looked at Logan with raised eyebrows. Apparently, he'd made a new friend.

Before he could introduce her or explain who this woman was, all three of them turned at the sound of footsteps coming up the trail from below.

"It's just us," Collin huffed and puffed.

"You sure sound out of shape for an FBI guy," Logan teased him.

Lucy took the opportunity to rest her head on his shoulder. She knew she needed to get up. They had a lot to do yet but now that the adrenaline was wearing off, she was exhausted.

Collin came into view a few paces behind some other older lady and bobbed his head in her direction, "It's more that she came sprinting up here without breaking a sweat." He looked at her in a combination of frustration and admiration. Then he leaned his hands on his knees and caught his breath for a moment.

Logan took that opportunity to introduce Lucy.

"Well, yeah, I kind of assumed the woman jumping to your defense and then curling up in your lap would have to be Lucy," the redhead replied sardonically. Then, seeing that Lucy was working her way up off Logan's lap, the redhead stuck out her hand to offer assistance while adding, "I'm Geri, and that's Joan. We came to rescue you, but you seem quite capable of rescuing yourself."

"I just completely lost my shit," said Lucy. It was embarrassing how true that statement was, but Geri just laughed.

"Oh, honey, that's completely normal. I'd be more worried if you didn't. Now, what exactly happened? You said something about killing someone."

Collin sucked in a loud breath and looked at Lucy with wide, questioning eyes.

"Shit," she thought. He was going to have to arrest her, wasn't he?

She could lie, but Jenn and Frank were both witnesses, so it would be two against one.

LOGAN

He'd stood up and dusted himself off once Lucy was standing, but he didn't like the way she was looking at the ground now. She scuffed her toe in the dirt and moved away from him.

"It was self-defense, Collin. You get that, right?" There was no chance in hell he'd let Lucy end up in trouble for any of this mess.

"Yeah," Collin was studying Lucy closely. "Give me the short version. Then we'll head back to the car where I might have enough reception to call it in. If I can't get a call through, we'll need to drive out to somewhere."

They all turned to look at Lucy. When Logan saw her shoulders slump forward, he moved closer to her and wrapped an arm around her.

She turned into him and straightened up to kiss his cheek before stating firmly. "I'm okay."

"I know, but I'm here no matter what."

She gave him a smile that lit his heart on fire.

Then she looked back to everyone else, took a deep breath and explained about being surprised by the ice machine and then coming to in the old barn. She told them about wriggling free of the rope, slashing at Frank and stabbing Jacob in the throat. Her summary finished with her chasing Jenn down the trail and seeing her attacking Logan.

"Okay, we can work with that. Where's your knife now?" Collin asked her.

Lucy gave him a terrified look. Logan was relieved when Geri spoke up, "She doesn't know where. She fought off three lunatics. It's somewhere between here and the barn or with one of them."

"Fair enough. We'll need to find it at some point. Who tied up Jenn?"

While Logan had been trying to calm Lucy down, he'd noticed Jenn starting to crawl away. Before she got far, Geri had moved in, pulled a couple zip ties from a pocket running down the thigh of her pants and zipped Jenn's wrists together behind a thin but tall tree. Jenn was still in that same spot, stewing furiously and sputtering wordlessly.

"Ok, Logan, I'm going to give my phone to you. I need you, Joan, Betty, and Linda to find a signal, call our backup and get them here. Geri, Lucy, and I will drag Jenn, here, back up to find Frank and Jacob."

"Lucy should come with me," Logan was not prepared to let her go again. He really wanted to borrow some of Geri's zip ties to connect Lucy to him so that nothing else bad could happen to her without him being there, too.

The apologetic look on Collin's face told him this would be something he had to fight for. He geared himself up to argue his case, but Collin stole it all away from him.

"I hear you, Logan, but I need her to stay with me to show me around and explain what happened. I can't send her off with you to find a signal, but I need you to be the one to reach out to my backup. I get that you don't want to leave her, but this is the way it needs to happen."

Then he gave Logan the "I know you know I'm right" look that always made Logan want to punch him in the face. Granted, that look came with the fact that Collin usually was right, and Logan did know it. He just didn't like it.

He turned to Lucy. If she wanted him to stay with her, Collin could stick it in his ear. Logan wasn't leaving her unless she was okay with it.

"No matter what he says, I can stay with you, if you want." He looked right into Lucy's big brown eyes. Fuck, he loved her. It just kept hitting him. Lucy looked right back at him, and he knew she'd turn him down.

She cupped her hand around the base of his skull to pull his head down toward her as she lifted up on her toes to kiss him. It wasn't the brisk brush of her lips he'd felt on his cheek earlier. This was a real kiss. The kiss where she licked at the seam of his lips and begged him to return her passion. When she was satisfied with all that he'd given her, she let her heels collapse back to the ground. Then, with her hand still holding onto the back of his neck, she told him exactly what he expected to hear, "Y'all go call for help. I'll be fine with Collin and Geri."

Then she leaned up just long enough to grace him with a final brush of her lips against his before pulling away from him entirely.

"I'll be here," she promised.

"I'll be back."

She started to turn away, but Logan put his hand on her elbow just above her brace, "Hey, I love you." He needed to be sure she knew.

"I love you, too."

"You need to go." Stupid Collin was right again. The sun was setting quickly now. He'd be lucky to make it back to the car before full dark. "Here's my phone. Just use the call history to dial the last number called. He'll connect you with the local agents already heading our way."

Geri pulled a headlamp from one of the bazillion pockets of her pants and handed it to him. It was almost as small as a nine-volt battery, but it lit the path in front of him well.

"What about all of you?" Logan and Joan were headed back to a car with light, and he had Collin's phone. The others were headed deeper into the woods with a lunatic to find a dead body and an injured psycho.

Geri grinned at him and pulled out a petite Maglite, "I've got us covered."

He felt stupid for continuing to be surprised by her. He couldn't even accuse her of looking like a sweet little old lady. She really did look more like a wild-haired, oddly competent homeless woman.

"Thanks." There really wasn't anything else for him to say to her.

"Oh, and tell them there's opium poppies involved," Geri added.

Logan and Collin both turned to look at her, but Collin spoke before Logan could form the words, "I'm sorry, what?"

"I think I figured it out. Or at least part of it. There's no time to explain it all now, just tell them about opium poppies."

"Yeah, ok." Logan didn't know what else to say, so he turned and headed down the trail with Joan right behind him.

Behind him, he heard Collin's voice, "You will explain it to me once we get to the barn and get everyone settled."

Chapter 22

LUCY

Collin shook his head as he used another set of Geri's zip ties to refasten Jenn's hands in front of her after removing her from the tree. Lucy would have preferred to see her hands behind her back, but she understood how dangerous that would be while they were still hiking.

Other than an occasional grumble, Jenn was mostly refusing to speak. It allowed them all to focus on their footing as the trail grew darker and darker. Collin and Jenn led the way with Geri in the middle shining the flashlight in front of all of them. Lucy followed closely behind Geri.

By the time they entered the small clearing around the barn, the sun had completely disappeared and taken all traces of orange and yellow and red along with it.

Lucy heard Frank before she could see him, "You," huff, "stupid," huff. Geri's shoulders were shaking with laughter as Lucy moved around her to see what was going on. Frank had evidently been working hard to drag himself out of the barn, but now he had straw and dirt and chunks of rotted wood and sawdust sticking to him all over. It was especially noticeable where it stuck to patches of blood that were becoming tacky as they started to dry. He looked like a scarecrow that had been run over.

Geri's laugh finally escaped her mouth as she taunted him, "What did you think you were going to do, Frank? Crawl all the way down the hill and what? Drive away? We always knew you weren't the sharpest tool in the shed, but this is a whole new level of stupid."

Then Frank vomited a small pile of white froth on the ground in front of him. His arms were shaking, and he was sweating. Lucy was relieved he wasn't looking at her. All his vitriol had been aimed at Jenn, who was still standing silently next to Collin. He passed her off to Geri with instructions to tie her to a tree. Then he went to check on Frank who was no longer conscious.

Collin studied Frank closely, but then he snapped his head over to Geri with a very pointed, "I think now would be a great time to explain the opium you mentioned."

"Huh, yeah, probably so. Should we drag him back into the barn first?"

Immediately, the image of Jacob's body popped into Lucy's vision. She did not want to go back in there.

"It's okay, Lucy. We're going to stay out here. Why don't we find a place for you to sit down?" Maybe she'd said something aloud, or maybe she'd turned white. Either way, Collin had come to check on Lucy.

She was pretty sure he wanted her to sit directly on the bare ground, but it was dark now. Dew might not be forming yet, but it wasn't completely dry up here to start with. She hated the feeling of a wet seat. She scrunched up her nose, "No, I'll be fine standing."

"Alright, I'm going to look around for a minute, but I'll be back soon." Then he turned to Geri. "Can you keep an eye on Frank? I think it's better if we don't move him. This looks like detox from opioid abuse to me." He raised an eyebrow at Geri who nodded back at him in agreement.

"I'll explain my suspicions when you're ready," she volunteered.

"I'd like to borrow the light for a few minutes first. Then we can settle in and talk. We'll be waiting for a while for the others to arrive." He nodded his head toward the barn to silently let Geri know what he needed the light for. Lucy refused to think about why he needed to go look around inside the barn.

Instead, she spent a few minutes breathing. She looked at the moon with clouds passing in front of the tiny sliver that was just starting to show. It wasn't even a quarter moon yet. She was amazed by how few days it had been since she'd been dropped off at the VT nine trailhead. She watched stars flicker on and off as the wind blew a filter of weather across her view of the universe. Then Lucy closed her eyes and listened. The trees whispered their song of reassurance to her while the sounds of crickets and owls and other night critters reminded her that mother nature marched forward through trials, tribulations, life, and even death.

When she heard footsteps, she refocused enough to check that Frank's chest was still moving up and down despite his silence. Jenn didn't appear to have the same concerns about sitting on gross, wet ground, and had resigned herself to a peaceful silence, even if she was making awful pouty faces. Geri, on the other hand, was staring at Lucy.

Lucy frowned at her.

"I was just thinking that you'll be okay," Geri said. "You should come join Betty, Linda, Joan, and me for lunch sometime. The meal doesn't always end with this level of adventure, but we usually get up to enough trouble to bring some excitement into our lives."

"Really?"

"We've only been arrested a few times, and the judge is sweet on Linda, so he always gets them to drop the charges and let us go."

Lucy raised her eyebrows. This woman was nuts. But she also sounded like fun. And she could picture Betty coming up with all kinds of craziness to get them into trouble.

"See, that's what I mean," Geri added, "as soon as you started to think it through, you realized how much fun we can be."

"I don't like the looks on your faces. What are you two plotting, now?" Clearly Collin had already discovered Geri's penchant for trouble.

Then he dropped a pile of straw on the ground in front the tree beside Lucy and invited her to sit. It would keep the cold of the earth from seeping into her backside, while giving her a dry and mostly soft spot to relax. It looked clean. She didn't have any interest in looking too closely at it. Instead, she simply told him, "Thanks," and sat down.

"Is Jenn secure?" he asked Geri while sitting himself down beside Lucy.

"Yeah, she finally wore herself out and is starting to snore, so I think we're good." Geri came to join them.

"So, about the purple flowers being opium poppies..." Collin prompted Geri.

Geri sighed but started explaining her suspicions.

LOGAN

Moving back down the trail had gone quickly, so there were still streaks of pink and orange across the sky as he and Joan crossed the clearing to find Betty and Linda sitting on the hood of Betty's car. He pulled out Collin's phone and crossed his fingers that the single bar showing would be a strong enough signal to get a call through.

When it wasn't, he may have stomped his foot and started swearing. Linda and Betty just laughed at him, but Joan offered the helpful tip of stepping closer to the cabin.

"Sometimes work crews put a booster in the house as soon as possible so they can get a signal. I don't remember if Frank and Jacob said anything about being able to call from here, but it wouldn't hurt to try."

Oh, thank the heavens! When he got to the far corner of the cabin, the signal jumped to two bars and let the call connect.

It took some talking to get S.A.C. Franklin to give him the direct line to the local agents, but he got it. Apparently, Special Agents Williams and Carlson were on their way.

"Agent Carlson."

Logan really wanted to be irritated by the gruff answer, but he'd heard Collin answer his phone the exact same way so many times he assumed they had to be required to take an entire FBI course on it.

"This is Logan Miller, I'm in Vermont with Special Agent Collin Warner. We found the woman, along with the people who took her. Collin has all of them up in a barn in the woods. We need you to come here to help."

"Why isn't Warner with you?" Logan figured Carlson knew enough about the area to understand the lack of signal in many places.

"One of the guys is injured and another is dead. We couldn't carry them down the trail. He has the third person restrained in zip ties."

"Hmm. We're already in Bennington, so just let us know where you are, and it shouldn't take us long to get there."

Logan realized he had no idea where they were and couldn't get any of the ladies' attention because he was on the other side of the house. "Hold on a second," he said into the phone before hitting the mute button and screaming, "Beeeetttttttyyyyyyyy."

Linda may be mostly deaf, but he knew Joan and Betty should be able to hear that. Just a minute later, Betty popped around one corner and Joan came around the other. Both had guns drawn and were looking very serious.

"It's all fine," he assured them, "I just need an address."

Both women deflated like released balloons as they lowered their weapons and came closer. "There is no address here. It was never assigned one. I mean, I guess technically, the new emergency system would dictate what it would be, so it does kind of have one, but it's not posted or recognized or anything. I'm not even sure if they've named this road."

Logan forced himself to ignore the 'new' system that had been implemented more than twenty years ago and asked, "Can you give them directions from Bennington?"

"Oh yeah, sure," Betty held out her hand for the phone.

After a few minutes of instructions like, "turn left by the old Parker place," that Betty followed by huffs of frustration when he must have pointed out that didn't mean anything to them, Betty complained, "These people don't know anything. You try," and handed the phone to Linda, who had come around the house to join them as well.

"I don't hear so good, so you just listen. You take VT nine east..." and off she went without pause. At least her directions seemed to be based on more recognizable landmarks rather than who owned the property back in the day. After finishing with, "You just keep going till you find us and the new construction at the end of the road. I'm giving you back to Logan, now," she handed him the phone.

"Did you get all that Special Agent Carlson?"

"Yeah. Williams is familiar enough with the area to have a good idea of where we're going. She didn't know about any new construction up that way, though."

"I would take their definition of 'new' with a grain of salt. It doesn't sound like anyone's been working on it since twenty eighteen."

"That makes more sense then," Logan heard the feminine voice that must belong to Williams coming through from their speakerphone.

"We'll be there in twenty minutes or so."

Logan said his goodbyes and hung up. He really wanted to go back up the trail to find Lucy and Collin, but it was fully dark now, and he didn't want to just abandon Joan, Betty, and Linda.

They all headed back to the cars as Joan apologized again for the transgressions of her grandsons. Linda kept telling Joan that it was the drugs. No one could account for what a person would do when they were on drugs, even though Joan kept swearing her grandsons weren't doing drugs. Finally, the bickering drove Betty crazy enough for her to intervene, "Enough! It doesn't matter. We don't know anything about what's going on. We just need to wait for the other agents, so we can show them the way up the trail."

"Can I ask you all something while we wait?" Logan was hopeful Linda, Betty, and Joan would be willing to spill the tea on Geri's background.

"I believe you just did, sir, and it did not require our permission for you to spit it out. Now, if you are wondering if we'd be willing to answer a question, that will depend on the question." Sometimes Betty sounded like a normal old lady; sometimes Betty sounded like an army general; and sometimes, like right now, it was obvious that she'd spent most of her life as a teacher. Logan twitched at the thought of accidentally asking, "*Can* I go to the bathroom?" instead of "*May* I go to the bathroom?"

Then he remembered all of Geri's hidden pants pockets stuffed with zip ties and flashlights and the secret arsenal she stored in the place of her spare tire. His curiosity outweighed his aversion to being corrected by a teacher.

"Okay," he started, "What's Geri's background? She's clearly got some special skills."

He'd known it had to be interesting, but the way the three women looked at each other made him wonder just how interesting it could be.

After a moment, they came to a silent agreement and turned back to him. He was surprised when Linda was the one to speak up. Despite being hard of hearing, she kept her voice to a low whisper, and Logan had to lean in to hear her clearly.

"We don't know much about the details. I went to high school with her, but we weren't really friends. She was always a bit different. She wore jeans and a black t-shirt every day. Mind you, this was back in the nineteen seventies. On top of that, she never dated and never went to any dances or anything. There were rumors that her dad was sometimes mean and other times overly friendly. No one really knows exactly what went on in her house, but Geri left town the day after our high school graduation.

A few years later, her mom killed her dad and then herself in a murder suicide. Geri showed up to deal with the aftermath. She decided to keep the house, though she had it totally renovated, and has been around off and on ever since. Before she retired, she worked for the State Department. She'd be gone for months or even years, and then show up for several months. When she was here, she started joining our book club. Well, we called it a book club, but mostly we just drank, hung out, and occasionally would go TP someone's house."

All three women laughed at that, and Logan imagined their whole crew sneaking through neighborhoods, half drunk, and carting rolls and rolls of toilet paper.

"Anyway, sometimes she'd get a lost look in her eyes, or she'd jump when there was an unexpected noise. She's never told us much about her work, but we all got the impression that she wasn't sitting behind a desk in an office in DC. She was a lot happier once she married Tom. They had quite a few good years together before cancer took him."

After that, the women took turns sharing stories about their "book club" shenanigans. It ended up taking Williams and Carlson closer to forty minutes to arrive, but they did make it, and the stories had made the time pass quickly.

The agents wanted the three older ladies to stay back at the cars, but, in unison, Betty, Linda, and Joan crossed their arms on their chests and cocked a hip to the side. Then Betty asked, "Just what do you plan to do to stop us from joining you?"

Logan watched Carlson debate handcuffing three little ladies to a vehicle while Williams chuckled. In the end, all six of them tromped up the trail to the barn. Betty retrieved another flashlight from her car and the agents each had their own, so they had adequate light to guide their way.

When they reached the clearing, Logan immediately spotted Lucy sitting on a pile of straw beside a large tree, her arms wrapped around her knees. The sight of her, safe, alive, and waiting for him, made his chest tight with relief. Collin was deep in conversation with the agents while Geri pointed toward the barn, explaining something with animated gestures. Frank was unconscious nearby, and Jenn sat zip-tied to a tree, looking sullen.

Logan made his way directly to Lucy, settling down beside her on the makeshift seat Collin had created. She immediately leaned into him, and he wrapped his arms around her, careful of her injured wrist.

"How are you holding up?" he asked quietly, his lips close to her ear.

"Better now that you're here," she murmured against his shoulder. "I keep thinking this should all feel like a nightmare, but somehow... it doesn't. Is that weird?"

Logan pulled back to look at her face in the dim light from the flashlights. "What does it feel like?"

Lucy was quiet for a moment, considering. "Like I found out who I really am. Like I found out who you really are." She paused, then added more softly, "Like I found out who we are together."

The simple honesty in her voice made Logan's heart race. "Tell me what you mean."

"When I was tied up in that barn, terrified and planning how to fight my way out, I wasn't thinking about getting back to my old life. I was thinking about getting back to you." She looked up at him, her eyes serious despite the exhaustion he could see there. "And not because I needed you to save me, but because I wanted to share whatever came next with you."

Logan felt something shift in his chest as he let go of subconscious worries about her leaving his life now. "I know exactly what you mean. When I thought I'd lost you, when I saw that empty tent... I was terrified. I couldn't imagine going back to my everyday life without you in it somehow."

"Is that normal?" Lucy asked with a small laugh. "To fall this hard this fast? To be so sure about someone after knowing them for less than a week?"

"I don't know if it's normal," Logan admitted, "but I know it's real. What we've been through together... most people don't experience that kind of intensity in years of dating. We've seen each other at our worst and our best. We've trusted each other with our lives."

Lucy nodded slowly. "I keep thinking about what you said earlier, about this not being trauma bonding. And you're right. This isn't us clinging to each other because we're scared. This is us choosing each other even when things are scary."

"Especially when things are scary," Logan agreed. He paused, then asked the question that had been nagging at him since their reunion. "Are you worried about what happens when we get back to normal life? When there's no adrenaline and no life-or-death situations?"

"Honestly?" Lucy shifted to face him more fully. "I think that's when we'll really get to know each other. But Logan, I'm not afraid of normal with you. I'm excited about it. I want to see what we're like when we're arguing about what to watch on Netflix. I want to know how you take your coffee in the morning and whether you hog the covers at night."

Logan laughed softly. "For the record, I do hog the covers, but I make excellent coffee."

"See? That's useful information for building a life together." Lucy's smile faded into something more serious. "Because that's what I want, Logan. I want to build a life with you. Not because of what happened here, but because of who you are. Who we are together."

"What would that look like?" Logan asked, his heart racing at the direction of their conversation.

"I don't know all the details yet," Lucy admitted. "But I know I want to wake up next to you. I want to go on adventures together and support your career and maybe figure out how to blend our lives without losing the independence I've worked so hard to find."

Logan cupped her face gently, mindful of the cuts and bruises she'd sustained. "I love you, Lucy. Not because you saved yourself, not because you're the strongest person I've ever met, but because you're you. Because when I look at you, I see home."

"I love you too," she whispered, leaning into his touch. "I love your kindness and your determination and the way you see the best in people. I love that you let me be strong while still wanting to take care of me."

They sat in comfortable silence for a moment, watching the FBI agents work around them until Collin's voice carried across the clearing, "Logan, Lucy. We're ready for your statements now."

Logan stood and helped Lucy to her feet, keeping one arm around her as they walked toward the agents.

Chapter 23

LUCY

Geri had just finished her explanation when they saw lights flickering in the woods.

"Do you think it's them?"

Collin was the first to reply, "At the very least, it's Logan. I'm honestly surprised he's been gone this long. I assumed he'd be back up the trail and at your side the second he made the phone call. Though if they had to drive to get reception, that may still be the case."

There was clearly more than one light in the woods. Lucy knew Logan had waited for backup to arrive. "Really?" She couldn't help but wonder what Collin was thinking.

He had the audacity to huff at her before answering, "Yeah, Lucy. I've seen that man date women and flirt with women. I've even seen him with a few crushes, but never once have I seen him in love with a woman until you. That also means you should be careful with him. If I find out that you're playing games with him, I will come after you."

"I love him, too."

"Yeah, I know."

"Lucy," Logan was the first one to emerge from the tree line and called for her. She was too stiff and sore to leap up and run at him the way she wanted. Instead, she picked herself up carefully just in time for him to be standing right in front of her. "Are you okay?"

"Yeah, I'm fine. My entire body hurts, and I plan to sleep for a week once this is over, but I'm okay. We think Geri may have even worked out everything that's going on."

Two other people in suits moved up behind Logan, "We'd be interested in hearing about it." Then the man that had spoken turned to Collin and prompted, "You must be Special Agent Warner. I'm Carlson, and this is Williams. We were told this woman was involved and had been cuffed?"

Wait, what? Lucy startled in surprise. Why would she be cuffed? Oh, shit! She'd killed Jacob. She should be in cuffs. Why hadn't she thought about that? Lucy started to turn toward Collin so that he could cuff her.

"What the fuck? No, I said Jenn, the third person, was involved and cuffed. This is Lucy. She's the woman who was abducted. We found her. She's not involved. She's the victim!" Logan had turned to face the two new agents and was holding Lucy behind his back so she couldn't see them anymore.

Everyone's head swiveled to Geri when she cleared her throat, "To be clear," she held up one finger, "Lucy's a survivor, not a victim, and," she held up a second finger, "she found us as she was chasing Jenn down the trail after she escaped and took down both Frank and Jacob."

"Agents, meet Geri. I'm Special Agent Collin Warner up from Virginia. Thank you for coming out here."

"No problem. Can you tell us what's going on?" Williams moved forward while Carlson looked around and processed everything that was happening.

"Certainly. First and foremost, Frank is the unconscious guy on the ground. He's still alive, but we think he's struggling through withdrawal in addition to a few minor slices and stab wounds. There is one body in the barn belonging to Frank's younger brother, Jacob. Joan is their grandmother, so she can give you more information about them both. Jenn is the one moaning and groaning over by that tree. Apparently, your arrival was enough to wake her. She's a bit cranky about being caught. She's also the niece of the sheriff, just a head's up. I'll let Geri explain her theory, and then maybe we can all go find a more well-lit, indoor place with food and coffee to finish everything?"

"We'll need to process the scene," said Carlson.

"Do you have a way to light it up and the manpower to come do that now, in the dark, at ten o'clock at night?" Collin was starting to sound a bit snippy with the male agent.

"No, so you're right. We can all get more comfortable before taking full statements, but we also can't leave the scene unattended. Carlson, why don't you use the satellite phone to call in more people. This clearing should be enough for it to work up here."

Huh, the woman was the one in charge. Lucy liked her. The male agent could go lick a rock, though she did refrain from suggesting that to his face.

"I'll check out the inside of the barn, too." Carlson added, "Are you sure it's clear, Agent Warner?"

"Yes, but just holler if you want back up."

Once he walked off, Williams apologized for his attitude and explained that he was a city boy who hated being called out to the woods. Especially in the middle of the night.

"Let's start with just the basics. How did this whole thing start?" she prompted them while looking from face to face.

Lucy moved up beside Logan and gave her the brief version about spotting the flowers, finding the guns, and waking up lost with no gear.

"So, the flowers are important. I knew it," Logan threw in before explaining his own run-in with Frank and Jacob before getting lost and finding Lucy.

"Geri was able to identify the flowers, and I think her theory is certainly possible if not probable," Collin shifted their focus to Geri.

"Jenn's been working at the general store since she was in high school. Now that she's living on her own, she's been talking about starting her own shop selling tea and coffee. Gary, the store owner, let her start selling drinks in the general store, but it wasn't going well. No one around here's used to going out for tea or coffee. A couple weeks ago, she started offering her 'special tea.' It got popular quick, especially with the younger crowd, but soon even a lot of the adults started stopping by for a cup, sometimes every day. Everyone said it made them feel better. All their aches and pains would go away. I hadn't gotten around to trying it myself, but the girls and I had been talking about it."

As she started to digress, Collin redirected her, "Explain the flowers, Geri."

"Oh yeah, so Logan showed me a picture of them, and they look like poppies, but just a little different and purple. I'm used to the red ones. Anyway, there was an article a few years back about some farmer around here getting busted for growing a field of poppies for the opium. When I was at the library last week, I saw it laying on the top of a stack of papers in the records corner. Anyway, that and the picture of the flower reminded me about some people I used to know back in Asia who would use the seeds to brew opium tea. There were lots of poppies growing in that area, so it was a cheap and easy way to forget all their issues. Just one problem, the tea was inconsistent, so sometimes they ended up dying instead of flying." Geri laughed at her own play on words.

Lucy suspected her time in Asia connected to her familiarity with zip ties and comfort with weapons, but that would have to be another story for another day.

Williams didn't laugh with Geri, "That all does make sense, but I'm not sure I fully understand why they decided to do all this. Surely, they realized they were likely to get busted as soon as people started getting sick or dead from the tea."

"Ha, you're giving them too much credit, Special Agent Williams. Jacob is... well, was dumb as a box of rocks. He was infatuated with Jenn and wanted to be just like his older brother. He'd do anything they asked. Frank wasn't real bright himself, but he was always looking for stupid ways make a name and a buck for himself. I hadn't thought about it until now, but Jenn has been jacking up the price of the tea. She's been telling everyone that it's all locally sourced, dried, and she blends it herself, so as demand has increased, she's been saying she has trouble keeping up. I guarantee she's the mastermind of this whole thing. She's smart enough to recognize the value of customer loyalty when those customers are literally addicted to your product, but not quite intelligent enough to see the long-term trouble."

"It would have been fine. I made sure the tea was just strong enough to make people feel better. I was helping them. They could work more comfortably, and I was getting my business going. It was good for all of us. I knew that fool Frank shouldn't have planted them so close to the stupid trail, but no one was out hiking when he first got them started. Those idiots he was working with were just as bad. Who gives us guns we can't get ammo for, anyway?"

Williams walked over to Jenn, and asked, "Who was Frank working with?"

"Idiots from the city. They bring their drugs through here, and with elections coming up, local sheriffs like my uncle sometimes try to stop them. My uncle refuses to be bought off, but he loved my tea."

"So you're confessing, then?"

"No, I'd like a lawyer, and you haven't read me my rights."

Williams looked over at Collin for confirmation, and Lucy watched his face get a little darker, "Yeah, she's right. I haven't officially arrested her yet."

Williams' look of disappointment made even Lucy feel guilty. She hoped Collin wouldn't get in trouble.

"That explains the big picture, but how did everyone end up out here?"

Logan wrapped an arm around Lucy and jumped in to explain the way Lucy had recognized Jenn at the general store and then had been taken from the hotel.

"Alright, we'll do the rest in the morning. We'll set up shop at the sheriff's office. Can you all manage to bring yourselves in so we can get your full statements, or will I need to send someone after you?"

"We'll all be there," Joan's quick reply made Lucy think she might not be the only one Williams had made feel guilty.

"The body in the barn was slashed across the throat with the world's smallest knife. It was left lying on the floor beside the body. Anyone want to volunteer whose prints we'll find on it?" Carlson asked as he walked back up to them.

Lucy started to raise her hand, but Logan pulled it back down and wove his fingers in with hers.

Then Carlson rolled his eyes, "It looked like self-defense. No one would choose to launch an unprovoked attack with a knife that small. Obviously, we'll find out who it is anyway. I'm just trying to speed up the process a bit."

"It's okay, Logan. She can tell him," Collin's encouragement was enough for Logan to stay quiet while she explained about waking up hog-tied, getting free, and slashing at Frank before charging Jacob and hitting his throat. She wouldn't do anything differently. She firmly believed it had been her or them, but she was still crying by the time she finished.

"This was not the first incident between them," Collin added. "She also found a cache of weapons they had stored in the woods, which we believe led them to drug her and leave her in the woods with no supplies. Our best guess is that they were trying to make her look like a lost hiker who died out there."

Both the other agents turned back to Lucy with raised eyebrows. She was hoping they'd let her save that part of the story for tomorrow. She just didn't have any words left.

Carlson dashed those hopes when he kept his eyebrows high on his forehead while prompting, "We need to hear the story from the beginning."

"The short version is fine for tonight," Williams was trying to soften the blow, "but we do need to know what happened. It sounds like you can explain the guns our friend over there was talking about."

Before Lucy could even start, Logan jumped to her rescue, "Tomorrow she can use a map to show you where she found the guns. I found her empty tent and abandoned pack near Goddard Shelter. Frank was there, and when I asked him about the gear and if he'd seen Lucy, he attacked me." From there Logan explained running into her and their adventure back to the road. Even Betty chimed in to explain their meeting with the sheriff and his relation to Jenn.

By the time the full tale was told, Lucy had dried her tears and was feeling grateful to have found so many caring people willing to help her. Then Logan wrapped her in a hug, and Carlson and Williams dismissed them for the night. Carlson reassured Williams that he had a team on the way, and they'd both made it clear everyone would be interviewed more thoroughly in the morning.

LOGAN

The rest of the team must not have been too far away. By the time he, and Collin, and the ladies were all piling into their cars, there was a van and an SUV pulling in behind them. Geri, Linda, and Joan drove away while Betty waited patiently for Collin to brief the new arrivals before he climbed into her passenger seat.

Everyone had agreed to arrive at the sheriff's office at ten the next morning. It was after midnight now, and they all wanted showers and sleep. Collin would drive the three of them in. The ladies all had their own transportation arranged.

They'd thanked Betty profusely when she'd dropped them off at the hotel, but she'd been grinning and claiming it was the most fun she'd had in almost ten years, which made Logan feel better, but also had him wondering what all she'd done in her life more than ten years ago that had competed with the last two days.

As they entered the hall, Logan couldn't help but wonder, "Do you think the sheriff was in on it?"

"Nah, he was enjoying the tea himself, and even Jenn said he refused to be bought. I think his niece took full advantage of him, and he was certainly oblivious, but I don't think he was supporting it." Collin was confident in his answer and with his experience, Logan trusted him.

"So, what did they need the guns for if they were just growing flowers?" Lucy wondered. "And why keep the guns under a heap of leaves in the middle of the woods?"

Collin turned back to face them and cocked his head in thought, "It's not uncommon for people in this situation to have guns to protect an illegal crop. We often see it with fields of marijuana. The guys Frank worked with likely gifted him with the guns to help him protect their trade route. Were they in protective cases or anything when you found them?"

"No, just buried under leaves. I didn't even see any ammunition with them."

"That might be the answer. There are several types of ammo that are very hard to get right now, and Jenn commented something about weapons they couldn't get ammunition for. It's likely Frank and Jacob had other weapons that they were comfortable with and had plenty of ammunition for. If there's a larger organization behind this, there might be a lot of drugs coming in from the coast and being trafficked through this area. Having a community, including law enforcement, who are already users would make it impossible for them play any part in prosecuting the bigger dealers. It's more convenient than necessary, but if Jenn was already looking to get something started, it might have been a happy coincidence for those supplying her with the plants." Then Collin shrugged, "Carlson and Williams will get the joy of trying to untangle that web. Or they might pass it off to the DEA and walk away. Either way, I'm ready for bed."

Before Collin could turn to go up the stairs to his own room, Logan stopped him, "Hey, thanks. Seriously. I really appreciate you coming up here and everything you've done." He looked down at Lucy who was holding his hand and resting her head on the side of his shoulder. "It really means a lot to me."

Collin gave him a sad smile before answering, "I know, man. I'm glad I could be here for you. It's good to see you happy."

Collin was lonely. Logan had never thought about it before. He'd had no interest in getting involved with anyone himself, and he'd never bothered to notice his friend's desire for a relationship.

He didn't know what to say without sounding like a condescending dick, so he didn't say much at all. He just tipped his head at Collin and offered a final, "Thanks," before he steered Lucy toward their room. His memory of locking the door earlier that day was fuzzy, and he wasn't entirely sure he had a room key with him, but they could go to the front desk if they needed to.

The detour to the front desk proved unnecessary when he opened his wallet and their room key fell out. Lucy picked it up, though her slight sway as she stood up told him everything he needed to know about just how tired she was.

Once he got them both in the door, he stripped them both down, gently removed her wrist brace, and ushered them into the shower. He kissed every scrape, scratch, and bruise he found as he gently scrubbed her clean. Her left wrist had been protected by her brace, but the deep marks around her right wrist and both ankles would likely display every color of the rainbow before they healed. As he dried her off, and escorted her over to the bed, he quietly promised to be there to kiss every single color change of those bruises.

She murmured back to him that she wasn't going anywhere either and added that she liked Pennsylvania. He'd been prepared to move to Tennessee or wherever she wanted to be, but her moving to Pennsylvania suited him just as well.

Then Logan laid on his back and enjoyed the feeling of Lucy's breath ghosting across his chest as she snuggled into him. It didn't take long for her breaths to slow down and even out, and then her snoring began. He loved it. Every sound and tickle of his chest hair was the perfect feeling he'd never known he was missing.

EPILOGUE

L ucy stopped and sat on the bridge. It was hard to believe it had been more than a year since she was last here. She pulled off her pack but paused before getting out her water filter and heading down to the creek. For just a moment, she sat and listened.

Unlike last time, there was no unnatural stillness or silence. She heard birds chirping, wind rushing through the trees, and a squirrel scampering around somewhere in the distance. It was still early in the morning, and she noticed three deer were tucked back into the trees munching on leaves while keeping an eye out to see what she was doing.

She smiled when she also heard footsteps and the quiet clack of trekking poles. Logan "Jacks" claimed that he wanted her to lead because she was the better navigator, but when the path is as well-established as the Appalachian Trail, there wasn't much need to navigate. Lucy knew the real reason Jacks liked to follow her instead of lead. He still loved the view of her backside. She assumed it helped motivate him to hike a bit faster and keep up with her. After everything that they'd been through together, it really didn't matter who led and who followed. At the end of each journey, they stood side by side, just as they would when they finished their thru-hike of the Appalachian Trail by summitting Mt. Katahdin in Maine.

They hadn't expected it to be easy to find someone willing to climb to the top just to marry a couple of smelly hikers who'd been living in the woods for six months, but Collin had been thrilled with both the idea and the adventure. He'd gotten his license so that he could officiate the ceremony. They just needed to let him know what day to meet them there. Collin was planning to book a whole week in one of the cabins in Baxter State Park as soon as they told him when.

After they'd filled out extensive paperwork and answered the same twenty questions fourteen thousand times for the FBI, Lucy had become accustomed to thinking of the man she loved as having two names. When they were in civilization, he was Logan. But when they left the asphalt and entered the trail, he became "Jacks." He still carried a set of jacks with him on every hike, and over the last few months, she'd gotten pretty good at it herself. She'd even beaten him a few times.

The trail name "Loner" no longer fit her. She started the trail without a name, but soon everyone was calling her "Lady Jacks" both because of her determination to learn the game and give Jacks a run for his money, and because the two of them were rarely seen without one another.

They'd moved in together almost immediately after they'd gotten off the trail last year. That attempted hike had already felt like a bookend to her round of adventures, and she had been trying to decide what she wanted to do next. After everything that happened on that trip, relaxing in his comfortably messy house in Pennsylvania while continuing her freelance work had felt like the perfect next step.

Neither of them had escaped Vermont unscathed, though her physical wounds had healed quickly. They'd both experienced nightmares, but they woke each other up and talked about them and healed together. He understood her worries and never made her feel silly for things like keeping an extra-large survival kit in her car or carrying a GPS tracker with her everywhere she went. Six months of therapy had helped and given her a toolbox full of coping skills, but it would take time to fully move forward.

For her birthday, Logan had bought Lucy a fancy, new mini-tracker that she wore like a bracelet, and she'd put it on without a single word about his need to always know where she was. He showed no interest in controlling anything about her life. The account to track the bracelet showed he logged in only once to set up his account and password, but she knew how important it was to him to be able to find her if he ever needed to. That was Logan's nightmare, that he would arrive to find her body instead of Jacob's. So, she wore his bracelet every day and treasured knowing that someone loved her enough to always come looking for her when she got lost or needed help. His therapist had checked that she was okay with it, and then labeled it as a mostly reasonable coping mechanism.

It had been around three AM one night after she'd had trouble sleeping that he brought up the idea of them getting back out there and finishing what she started. She'd loved the idea. There was no way she was willing to sacrifice her independence or spirit of adventure because of all they'd been through. Both of them had started this journey before, but neither of them had been able to complete it, so now they'd do it together.

Logan and Lucy loved the trail too much to join the high-impact crowd that started at Springer Mountain in Georgia in the spring. They'd decided to flip-flop. They started in the middle of the trail at Harper's Ferry, WV and hiked south to Springer. Then they'd flown to Myrtle Beach for a weeklong vacation before returning to Harper's Ferry and continuing north.

It was at the beach that Logan had proposed to her. Collin had come to meet them for dinner to celebrate. That was when he'd agreed to officiate for them when they finished their hike. Now, they were less than six hundred miles from their wedding day. They were guessing it would be six or seven weeks, but they weren't in a big hurry. They'd made good time, and it was still July. Lucy was expecting a September wedding with fall colors in the background.

Logan came up beside her then and took the water filter from her hands while kissing her senseless. "Whatcha thinking about, Beautiful?" Then he wiggled both eyebrows in the most comically flirtatious way she'd ever seen.

"Our wedding. It'll likely be as the fall colors peak in Maine, I think."

"And they still won't hold a candle to you."

Lucy laughed, "Go get water, you sexy stud. I'll pull out snacks."

"There's a bag of peanut M&Ms stashed in my hip pocket," he called over his shoulder as he climbed down the bank to get water.

Jacks hated peanut M&Ms but he bought a bag at every resupply stop, because he knew Lucy loved them. She didn't need him to bring snacks for her, but she loved that he did it anyway.

Two hurricanes collide, destroying the Appalachian Trail and bringing together two hearts, but only if they can survive together, in Crossing with Kiara.

Romantic Suspense Fiction

Taylor Industries:

Rural romantic suspense with international intrigue
Linked Hearts
Encrypted Hearts
Tracking Hearts
Guarded Hearts
Auditing Hearts
Hacking Hearts

Twisted Willow:

Small town romantic suspense full of action & adventure
Gloria's Gumption
According to Cora
Beth's Absolution
Letting in Liz

On-Trail Love Adventure:

Romantic suspense on the Appalachian Trail
Alongside Lucy
Standing by Stephanie
Crossing with Kiara

Nonfiction

The Truly Successful Author
The Truly Successful Writer

About the Author

Selfie of the author in the wild.

Follow me on Instagram for behind-the-scenes sneak peeks and hints at what's to come.

Subscribe to my newsletter to be the first to hear about new releases, get special discount offers, and access bonus material, including Geri's Journey for free!

Maria lives in the woods and loves hiking, reading, and writing. Her first completed work was a play about her family's crazy holiday adventures. It was written in pencil on wide-ruled paper. Maria was 8. Since then, she's worked in restaurants, gone to college, taught middle school, published some stuff, written scary amounts of online content, and hiked sections of the Appalachian Trail.

When she can't go enjoy an adventure, she writes one down on paper. They usually involve the woods and hot, loving men who support strong women. She's lucky enough to be married to a man willing to cook dinner and care for the dogs when Maria gets too sucked into the story in her head to remember the world around her.

Connect with Me

Scan me to connect!